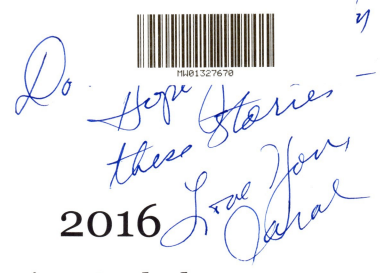
2016

Spring Anthology

By Little CAB Press

A TIME TO BLOSSOM:

Stories of triumph over adversity

2016 Spring Anthology by Little CAB Press

A TIME TO BLOSSOM: Stories of triumph over adversity

Published by Little CAB Press www.littlecabpress.com

Published in the United States of America

ISBN- 10:0692710817

ISBN- 13:978-0692710814

Proverbs 3

5 Trust in the Lord with all thine heart; and lean not unto thine own understanding.

6 In all thy ways acknowledge him, and he shall direct thy paths.

Contents

From the Publisher:
A LETTER TO MY CHILDREN

Please do not ever allow the dislikes and annoyances that you may feel for one another to ever come between you being an eternal union of brothers and sisters. Be tolerant and forgiving, be quick to love and forgive and slow to judge and be angry. Remember Christ's teachings when you are dealing with your family so that during the most important and crucial times of each of your lives, you can rely upon and help each other. Look to your future spouses to be an addition to your family unit rather than an escape from it. Our family will grow; new people will come into it through marriages and births, let us rejoice together and love each other and be each other's very best and most trusted friends. Follow these guidelines with each other and our family will be eternally strong—

Honesty: Be honest with yourself and with your family; be truthful and trustworthy. Lies breed dissent and mistrust and they show a lack of respect for one another.

Respect: Respect your siblings and their future spouses and future children as children of God and never allow your words or actions toward them to be offensive or make them feel as though you are their enemy.

Trust: Share your life with your family so they know they are a part of you and have a share in your welfare; share everything so they can trust you.

Friendship: Be each other's best friends, be on each other's side, always there for one another through everything; the most trusted friends. Do not put the friendships of others above your family relationships.

Unconditional Love: Show a Christ-like love. Always be there for each other no matter what, even when mistakes are made; be quick to forgive and quick to offer unconditional love.

Gather: Gather together often for holidays, vacations, special occasions and include everyone and be welcoming to every member of the family.

Prayer: Always pray for God's help and blessings upon each other!

I love you my children! Please love one another forever!

WORTH OF A SOUL
By A.P. Maddox

Late afternoon sunlight spilled through the westward facing, floor length windows like waterfalls pouring the sun's rays into the gymnasium. Ben Willcox sat at the edge of the bottom bleacher eating his sandwich from his brown paper bag—his broom leaning at rest for the moment by his side.

The click-clack sound of high heeled shoes stepping across the gym floor drew his attention upward and he watched as a young woman approached. She was slender and neatly attired—her dress the color of a clear blue sky—and her long, blond pin curls cascaded over her shoulders.

He stood as she drew near—for he had been raised to always stand in the presence of a lady. Ben was a tall young man; at six foot two inches, he stood nearly a foot above the young woman. He was muscular and dark haired with a strong jaw line.

She stopped in his shadow and smiled up at him, his frame blocking the sun's rays around her. "Hello Ben," she said, reaching into her bag. "I'm in your world studies class." She produced an apple and held it out to him.

He nodded. "Your name is Audrey Hughes, right?" he asked, giving a puzzled glance toward the apple.

"You know my name!" she said with a smile. "I didn't think you would have noticed me. Would you like the apple?"

"Well, sure," he agreed slowly, "but I don't understand ma'am, why are you bringing me an apple?" Ben was reluctant but gently took the apple from her hand.

"Do you mind if I sit?" she asked.

"Oh sure, um, please do," he stammered, motioning to the bleachers. "Please pardon me ma'am, I forgot my manners."

They sat down together as she said with a smile, "Please, call me Audrey."

He returned a shy, slight smile to answer, "Alright then, Miss Audrey. But is there something I can do for you?"

"Oh, no," she replied. "I just pass by this gym sometimes and often see you eating your sandwich—bologna is it—and thought you'd like something different for a change."

"Well, I thank you Miss Audrey, but it sure isn't necessary," he said, trying to hand the apple back to her.

She wrapped her delicate fingers around his to gently push the apple back toward him. "Please take it," she said softly.

He retracted his hand. "Well, thank you then," he said, hanging his head slightly. He couldn't understand why this beautiful young woman— whom in class had all the attention she could ever want from both male would-be suitors and female friends alike—would bother to single him out by bringing him an apple. Did he look needier than he really was? Perhaps she believed him to be a charity case.

After a quiet moment she put her hands in her lap, sat up tall and began to chatter. "I have to say, you have such a brilliant mind!" She stopped to smile at him and went on. "I love to listen to you in class; you seem to know more than Professor Campbell does about nearly every country in the world! Where did you learn such wonderful things?"

Ben nodded, he understood now—she needed help with the class work. "I just really like encyclopedias and atlases," he told her, shrugging. "I could study them for hours. We didn't have many books at home but when I'd go into town with my dad, I'd head straight to the library and pour over the atlases and encyclopedias until dad came to pick me up again."

Looking over at her, he caught her gaze. Her blue eyes were bright and seemed to have a smile all their own. "If you need help with the class work," he slowly continued, a little mesmerized by her stare, "I can show you the best books in the library to study and research from."

"That'd be wonderful," she said with a happy sigh, noticing how deeply mysterious his green eyes were. "But I hope you don't think I came here just to pick your brain."

"Why then?" he asked, furrowing his brow.

"Would it be alright," she asked hesitantly, "if I said, I just wanted to get to know you?"

They stared into each other's eyes for several long moments. Ben had seen Audrey twice a week in class since the beginning of his sophomore year at Central Community College and had thought from almost the first day she was one of the most beautiful girls he had ever—or would ever—see in his life. She was always so surrounded by both male and female company however that Ben never figured he would ever get the chance to even say "hello," let alone get to know her.

What he couldn't have realized however was that he, being a strikingly handsome young man despite his quiet manner, had caught Audrey's eye almost from the start. She had hoped sometime during the year he'd approach her, but it was now spring and the school year would be over in a few short months and she felt if he wasn't going to approach her then she must seek him out.

She was of course, a proper young lady, raised to believe men did the asking, so she had waited patiently but this was 1930 and the world was changing and she just felt she couldn't let him get away without trying.

"That'd be alright ma'am, um, I mean, Miss Audrey. That'd be fine," Ben slowly responded in surprise.

Audrey relaxed her shoulders and sighed in relief. Smiling triumphantly, she said, "Good! Let's start with where you're from..."

Ben nodded, drew a breath, raised his brow and slowly began, "Well, I'm from the east side of the valley. My dad has a farm there that was my granddad's before him and I grew up working it. I'm the oldest of seven kids, the rest are still at home and they all work the farm before and after school, just like I did. My dad works hard to provide for his large family and most of the time we have barely enough to get by but my dad encouraged me to come to school—to learn the 'modern way'—and then come home and teach him how to run the farm more efficiently, to turn a better profit. I do janitorial work here to pay my way and I work at the gas station over on 5th & Main and—I also tutor math."

"I knew about the gas station," she said. "I have seen you there, but I didn't know about the math. You must be very good at it then?"

Ben shrugged. "I suppose," he said. "It comes rather easy to me."

"That's wonderful," Audrey said smiling. "Do you have any students I know?"

"Most of my students are high school kids," he said. "But I do have a couple here as well."

She nodded and smiled. "You know, your dad sounds like a great man. To do without you so you could come here and get an education, that's wonderful of him" she said.

"He's the best," he quickly agreed with a proud smile. "Your turn Miss Audrey, where are you from?"

"Well, I'm from the upper west side," she told him. "My dad owns real estate, commercial properties, hotels, stuff like that. I have two sisters, both younger, but no brothers and I'm here—going to school—to get as much education as possible for whatever comes my way. Whether I end up working with my dad helping run his company one day or if I have the good fortune of getting married and raising a family of my own, I'm just taking as many classes as I can to prepare myself for whatever my future has in store." She stopped and smiled at him again before stating with a glimmer in her eyes, "I feel like the future is an unwrapped gift under God's Christmas tree and we're on the verge of Christmas Eve!"

Ben chuckled. "I like your enthusiasm."

Her smile heightened as she enjoyed watching him laugh.

The fast paced clomping of Ben boss—Mr. Stone's—footsteps across the gym floor interrupted the couple's enjoyment of getting to know one another.

"Oh no," Ben moaned, "how long have we been sitting here?"

"Oh about ten minutes," Audrey guessed.

Ben looked at his watch. "More like twenty," he said. "My break is only fifteen minutes and I was halfway into that when you came in."

Audrey put her hand to her mouth. "Oh dear, I've gotten you in trouble. I'm terribly sorry," she said.

"It's not your fault," Ben let her know. "I will have to get back to work now though."

Ben stood. Mr. Stone looked very angry.

"Break time is over!" Mr. Stone bellowed. "You're not getting paid any overtime and you certainly aren't getting paid to socialize! Miss, you'll have to leave."

"Yes sir!" the couple answered in unison. Ben picked up his broom to get back to work and Audrey turned to go but quickly spun back around.

"Can we see each other again," she asked quickly, biting her lip.

"Yes," Ben answered, nodding with a warm smile.

"When," she questioned.

"Tomorrow, lunch?" he suggested.

"The cafeteria?" she asked.

"Yes," he said breathlessly at the thought of seeing her again.

"Excellent," she said smiling and turning to leave.

As she walked away Mr. Stone began shouting. "What do you think you're doing? Sitting around gabbing with a girl when you're supposed to be working! Are you going lazy on me? We can give this job to someone else boy, if you don't want it!"

Audrey neared the door and glanced back over her shoulder to give Ben a look to let him know how terribly sorry she was. He returned a look to let her know all was well and they exchanged smiles.

"I'm very sorry Mr. Stone," Ben said. "It won't happen again."

"You're darned right," Mr. Stone growled, "because the next time you'll be fired!"

"Yes sir," Ben answered, getting back to work.

The next day Ben and Audrey met in the cafeteria as they had prearranged. Audrey had arrived first and sat with friends to pass the time. Ben walked toward her feeling slightly nervous.

"Look!" Audrey's friend Alice said, pointing. "Isn't that Ben Willcox?"

"Oh he's a handsome fella," her other friend Ruth said with a swooning expression. "But what's he doing in here? I've never seen him in the cafeteria before."

"Looks like he's headed straight for us," Alice said.

"Do I look alright?" Ruth asked, looking to Audrey while straightening in her seat and fluffing her curls.

As soon as Ruth looked at Audrey she saw the knowing smile across Audrey's face as she looked at Ben. Then looking at Ben and seeing the same smile on his face as he came toward Audrey, she slumped in her chair. "Of course," she said with a sigh, "he's coming for you!"

"Is there any guy you couldn't get?" Ruth moaned in complaint.

"Of course," Audrey said, turning to wink at her, "I couldn't get the guy that's meant just for you."

"Miss Audrey," Ben greeted with a nod as he stepped up next to their table.

"Hello Ben," she delicately returned with a smile. "These are my friends, Alice and Ruth," she said pointing to each in turn.

He nodded to one then the other. "Nice to meet you ladies," he said politely.

Alice smiled simply in return. "Nice to meet you Ben," she offered.

Ruth sighed and put her elbow on the table and her cheek to her fist. "You wouldn't happen to have a twin brother hiding out anywhere would ya?" she asked with a dreamy grin.

Ben's eyes widened and his face flushed red. "Um, no ma'am," he answered— a little embarrassed.

"Oh well," Ruth said with a disappointed sigh, "that's just my luck."

Audrey stood and motioned to an empty table. "Shall we?" she asked.

"After you," Ben insisted. He nodded to Audrey's friends. "Ladies," he said politely as they both turned to go.

"Did I get you into too much trouble yesterday?" Audrey asked as Ben pulled out a chair for her.

"Not at all Miss Audrey," he replied, taking a seat for himself.

"I'm so glad," she said with relief. "I was so worried."

Ben shook his head and told her, "Mr. Stone is just like that. He always seems angry at something. Has something to do with his son dying in the Great War, I believe."

"Oh that's awful," she replied remorsefully, "so many were lost in that dreadful war."

"Yeah," he agreed. "I guess I just don't really blame him for being the way he is when I think of what it'd be like to lose your own child."

"Yes, poor man," she added.

They sat quiet for a few moments, eating their lunch before Audrey said more cheerfully, "If we finish our lunch quickly, can we go to the library so you can show me your favorite books?"

Ben smiled. "I'd love to," he said.

They laughed a little and quickly finished eating, almost racing each other to be done, and then, off to the library they went.

He showed her many of his favorite pages in the atlases and encyclopedias, telling her all about what he knew of the larger wonderful world they lived in. She watched his face with wonder and couldn't help but smile, as he related what he knew so joyfully.

After some time he said, "It's your turn now Miss Audrey, what are your hobbies and talents?"

"Oh I don't know if I'm terribly talented at anything," she replied, "but I enjoy reading and I play the piano some and I sing a little."

"I'll bet you sing like a beautiful song bird," he said, looking a little longingly into her eyes.

She smiled at the compliment and had to look down to hide the flushing of her cheeks. "I guess," she said shyly, "if there aren't too many critics in the audience."

"I would love to hear you sometime," he added.

She felt a little breathless gazing at his face which bore a look of genuineness and a growing romantic interest.

"And so you shall," she answered, "at Easter time."

"Oh, are you going to be in a pageant?" he asked.

"No," she continued with a gleam in her eye, "I'm taking you home with me for Easter."

Ben's face grew red and he kindly objected. "Oh no, I couldn't impose on your parents," he said.

It suddenly struck his mind what it would be like meeting Audrey's father—a very wealthy man by all accounts—what would he think of a lowly farm boy having anything to do with his daughter. A sick feeling grew in the pit of his stomach. He nervously looked at his watch and was glad to see it was nearly time for their next classes to start.

"We should go," he said rather despondently at the new realization he may not be welcome in her father's home.

"Ben, what's the matter?" she asked as they stood to walk out of the library.

He thought for a moment about how to express what he was feeling. He drew a deep breath and told her, "Your folks sounds pretty fancy Audrey and I'm just not sure I'd fit in with your family. We might be barking up the wrong tree here."

Audrey took his large, masculine, hard-working hands into her delicate, small hands and pleaded, "Ben please don't think that way. My father isn't like that, my family isn't like that. They'd all like you, I know they would."

Ben shook his head. "All fathers are like that Audrey," he countered. "It's their job."

"No," she argued, "my father would see that you have a good heart and that you're a hard worker and he'd immediately see how intelligent you are and he'd like you for all the things you are—he wouldn't judge you for what you are not."

"I don't know Audrey," he said with a frustrated sigh, "maybe it's just too soon to talk about meeting parents and stuff."

She realized she had jumped the gun and nodded her head in agreement. "Of course," she said, "you are right. I'm really sorry. Look, Easter is a full month away, let's just see what happens. Can we do that?"

Ben relaxed a little and agreed with some hesitation, "Yeah, we can do that."

Audrey gave a quiet sigh of relief and smiled, then slowly asked, "So what are you doing for lunch tomorrow?"

Ben looked at her sweet, beautiful face and smiling eyes, his head told him to walk away and let her go find a rich boy to be with—someone to please her father—but his heart was having a hard time resisting. He smiled at her, he couldn't help it. "Having lunch with you if that's alright," he said.

"That was my hope," she said happily before turning to go.

Ben let out a heavy sigh. "What am I going to do?" he grumbled under his breath as he watched her walk away.

The pair ended up spending lunch together every day for the next two weeks. Each time Ben thought he should put an end to them seeing each other—for she was way out of his league—but he would look into her eyes and knew he just had to see her one more day, one more time.

They began spending more time together; meeting for dinner in the evenings several times a week and with each passing day he was falling in love and knew she felt the same. Ben had come to decide that instead of putting an end to their budding romance he would instead put his best foot forward and try to make a good impression on her father.

He sent his folks a letter to let them know he wouldn't be home for Easter. He told them all about Audrey and his plans to meet her family on Easter weekend. He was even beginning to look forward to the occasion.

Easter weekend was now just days away. Ben met Audrey for lunch as usual but Ben was not his usual self when he arrived in the cafeteria.

"Ben, what's the matter?" she asked, putting her hand on his.

"Audrey, I'm really sorry, I cannot accompany you to your folks this weekend," he told her.

"Oh Ben, please, we've been over this, my parents are going to like you, I know they are. Why are you bringing this back up?" she asked.

"It's not that," he said, "it's Mr. Stone. I assumed we'd have the weekend off, but he told me today that we'll be working."

"Working?" she asked, astonished. "Who works on Easter?"

Ben shrugged and went on, "He said something about some deep cleaning he does annually on Easter weekend, says he takes advantage of no one being around."

"I don't believe it," she said, perturbed. "Everything was planned so perfectly! Isn't there anything you can do? Ask him again, please, for me?"

Ben gently took her face in his hands. "Audrey, I wanted to go with you, I had even started looking forward to it, but without this job I can't pay for classes. I'm sorry, I have to stay," he said.

"Oh Ben," she cried with tears beginning to wet her cheeks.

He hated to see her cry. His heart ached to make her stop and see her smile return to her face. He leaned toward her, they had not yet had their first kiss, though he had wanted to, he leaned a little more. "Audrey," he whispered, "I'm sorry. I love you."

She gasped a little, this was the first he had spoken the words. "I love you too," she told him, breathlessly.

Then it came—their first kiss—soft, gentle and sweet. A kiss that told Audrey Ben would have been there, by her side, if only he could have.

The next day Audrey found herself outside Mr. Stone's office. She did not know yet what she was going to say but she was determined to try to gain his mercy and get Ben released from work for Easter weekend.

She knocked.

"Come in." A voice growled from the other side of the door.

She hesitated; maybe it was a mistake to try to talk to him. *No*, she thought, *I must try*. She straightened her shoulders and turned the handle to go in.

"Mr. Stone," she said with some timidity in her voice, leaving the door ajar for a quick escape just in case he became too angry at her presence.

He looked up from his desk. "You're the girl," he barked.

She didn't know what to say to such a remark. "Um, well, yes, if you mean I'm Ben's girlfriend, you're right sir," she said.

"You're the one distracting him from his work," he grumbled.

"Well, now hold on sir," she said defensively, "I don't think that's fair. I believe Ben has been giving one hundred percent to his job. I know there was that first time when I kept him over on his break for a few too many minutes, but it's never happened again."

"Hmm," he grunted, unable to argue. "What do you want?" he asked.

"Well, sir," she began, trying to sound confidant; "I would like to ask if there's any way you could let Ben get off work for the Easter weekend?"

"You want me to do all the work myself?" he asked angrily, standing up to face her. "Do you know how much has to be done? And you want me to let the only helper they'll let me have go off on a jolly vacation?"

She stepped back, her lip began to quiver and he turned his back to continue.

"Sure," he said sarcastically, "I'll just do everything all by myself so the boy there can go have fun with his girlfriend! Sure, sure, that's what I'll do!"

She could see he wasn't to be persuaded and turned to leave before tears began to spill out of her eyes.

"I don't want to be alone," he mumbled under his breath before she made it through the door.

She stopped and slowly turned around. "What?" she asked quietly.

"I didn't say anything! Just go, I'll let Ben have the weekend," he said. "I guess someone should enjoy it."

"Mr. Stone, please pardon me sir, I don't mean to pry but, it sounded like you said you didn't want to be alone," she said.

"And what of it?" he asked, his voice changing from that of an angry boss to a lonely man.

"Is that why you work on Easter weekend then? So you won't be alone and you'll have something to do?" she questioned.

He slumped back in his chair, sighing his response.

"But Mr. Stone," she said, placing a gentle hand on his shoulder, "you don't have to be alone. Don't you have any family you could go to?"

"Family?" he grumbled, "my son is dead and my wife is gone. I have no family."

"Oh sir," she said sadly, "I'm so sorry. I had heard your son died in the war but I didn't know your wife had passed also, what a terrible thing for you."

"She's not dead," he said. "She left me, we're divorced. Neither one of us handled the loss of our son very well and we grew distant from each other till finally, she went to live with her sister back east."

"Oh dear, that's terribly sad," she said. She thought for a moment. "You know, you still don't have to be alone Mr. Stone, why don't you come with us? Come spend Easter with me and Ben and my family."

"No, that's okay Miss," he said, regaining his composure. "I couldn't accept and impose upon your family."

"Oh no, no, it wouldn't be an imposition at all," she told him. "We have a huge home, you'd have a room all to your own and my parents wouldn't mind a bit—truly. I'll telephone them to let them know. They'll have everything ready when we arrive."

He shook his head. "It wouldn't be right Miss," he said.

"You're right," she agreed, a smile growing across her face. "It wouldn't be right to leave you alone. Have your things ready for the weekend Mr. Stone, my father's car will arrive at nine o'clock in the morning to pick us up."

"But," he uttered, trying to protest.

"No buts," she interrupted. "Meet us out in front of the student hall—nine o'clock sharp!" She smiled but nodded her seriousness, then turned and left before he could argue further.

That evening she had a note sent to Ben's dorm room which read:

Meet me out in front of the student hall at 9 a.m., be ready to go! Mr. Stone is letting you go for the weekend! And... he's coming with us.

Ben couldn't believe what he read. "That girl!" he said chuckling.

He met Audrey's smiling face the next morning a few minutes early with everything ready to go. He took her into his arms and lifted her off her feet for a spinning hug. She giggled as they twirled. He set her down and kissed her. "I do love you, Audrey!" he said.

"Oh Ben," she replied smiling, "I love you too."

"How did you do it, though?" he asked.

"Let me fill you in quickly before he gets here," she said. "He wanted to work the weekend so he wouldn't be alone Ben, so I talked him into coming along with us!"

"And that worked?" he asked.

"Well, I guess we'll see in a minute," she answered, raising her eyebrows and grinning with anticipation.

9 o'clock came and Audrey's father's touring car arrived but Mr. Stone didn't.

"Can we wait just a few more minutes?" she asked the driver.

"Not a problem Miss Hughes," he answered.

She paced the sidewalk and Ben told her to come and sit on the bench. She did for a moment but then got up again, folding her arms in frustration and pacing, again.

"He's not coming is he?" she finally said, turning to Ben and throwing her hands down by her side.

"Yes I am Miss," Mr. Stone said, coming up the sidewalk behind her. "Thank you for waiting for me," he said with a nod.

She sighed in relief. "I'm so glad you came Mr. Stone," she let him know. Then smiling cheerfully she nodded toward the car. "Now let's get going?"

"Yes ma'am," Mr. Stone responded with a hint of a smile growing across his face.

Ben stepped over and shook his hand to greet Mr. Stone. "Thank you for letting me have the weekend off sir," he said.

"Thank her kid," Mr. Stone said, nodding to Audrey.

Ben looked at her—she was alive with excitement for the upcoming weekend. He couldn't help but smile at her. He had come to realize over the past weeks that to look at her was to smile, like a natural reaction whenever she was near.

They loaded their bags into the car and started off toward the Hughes home.

They drove past the city buildings of the downtown area—the government offices, courthouse and police station—through the crowded department store and hotel lined streets and into the countryside.

They drove several long miles, through rolling hills and past tree lined streams. Finally they turned down the dirt drive to the Hughes's country estate, horses galloped in the field off the left to welcome them. Audrey pointed out her favorites and told Ben their names.

Their home was a large two-story square with a covered porch surrounding the whole. The gleaming white paint was a stark contrast to the rolling green landscape.

"We are here!" Audrey announced with a grin as they pulled up in front of the home.

"Very fancy," Mr. Stone said quietly under his breath.

Ben's eyes were wide, and he began to second guess if he was up to this. Was he a fool to think a poor farm hick could win over a man as wealthy as Audrey's father? Knowing he couldn't turn back now, he took a deep breath and exited the car, turning to offer Audrey his hand.

Her parents and sisters came out to great them with smiling faces but Ben's nervousness grew. He wondered how much Audrey's parents knew about him, did they know he was just a poor farmer from the other side of the valley. He wondered how long it would take her father to tell him to get away from his daughter.

Audrey ran to hug them, then waved Ben and Mr. Stone over.

Ben looked at her face, so happy, so beautiful. He took another deep breath, reminded himself how much he loved her and decided he was not going to lose her without a fight. He swallowed his nervousness, stuck out his hand and walked boldly toward Audrey's father. He gave him a firm handshake as Audrey introduced them.

"Ben this is my mother and father, William and Helen Hughes," Audrey said, beaming. "And my sisters, Rose and Annie."

Rose was eighteen and would be joining her sister at the college in the fall. Annie was fifteen and still in high school.

"I'm very happy to meet you all," Ben said.

"Oh I must have a hug," Mrs. Hughes said wrapping her arms around him. "We were so thrilled when Audrey told us she was bringing a friend home with her. And what a handsome friend you are!" she said, releasing him and patting his shoulders.

"Well, thank you," Ben said blushing with a boyish smile.

Audrey introduced Mr. Stone to her parents as well and they were all invited inside.

They were directed upstairs and shown to their rooms to put their things down. They were told they had just enough time to freshen up before lunch.

Several minutes later they all met downstairs again and sat around the dining room table for sandwiches and lemonade. Audrey and her family did most of the talking at first. She told them about her classes. Her sisters talked about their school and friends. Mrs. Hughes talked about her projects in working with some of the other women of the community to sew quilts and clothing for the less fortunate families in the downtown area.

Mr. Hughes didn't say much until he started to question Ben.

"So Ben," he began in monotone voice, "tell us about yourself."

Ben knew this was his moment of truth and had been preparing. He quickly glanced at Audrey as if to ask how much to tell. She gave him a knowing smile, 'Tell him everything,' her look seemed to say.

"Well, sir, I'm from the other side of the valley—the east side. My family farms and to be honest we barely get by at times. I'm working two jobs to pay my way through school," he said with some confidence but without any feigned arrogance.

"When I'm finished with school I plan to help my father improve his operation in such a way that he can modernize and turn a better profit."

Mr. Hughes bent his head to the side a little in contemplation. "Sounds like you're a hard worker then," he commented.

"He is," Mr. Stone said, speaking up. "He is the best worker the school has ever hired to help me. He reminds me..." Mr. Stone paused as he began to get a little choked up. He took a moment, cleared his throat and continued, "He reminds me of my own boy."

Ben's breathing elevated slightly and he felt a lump in his throat. He had no idea Mr. Stone thought that way about him. His eyes felt misty but he blinked before a tear could form. He gave Mr. Stone a nod of gratitude.

"I like that," Mr. Hughes said. "I like that very much."

"He's also a brilliant mathematician Father, and he's a student of the world," Audrey said. "I sometimes think he's knows more than our world studies professor."

Mr. Hughes nodded and replied evenly, "That's wonderful."

He sat quiet for a moment and then spoke in a reflective tone. "I haven't been wealthy all my life, you know. I haven't told you girls about my childhood but I feel it's time now."

He lifted his chin to look at each of his daughters in turn and then went on, "I came from the city streets. I never knew my father—my parents weren't married. My mother did odd jobs cooking and cleaning to keep us in a shanty with a couple other families who were in a similar situation as ours. She died though of tuberculosis when I was twelve and I took to the streets shining shoes and whatnot just to be able to eat. I was shining shoes for a wealthy man out in front of a bank one day and he asked after my family. I told him I had none, so he asked me if I was honest and I promised him I was—for I had never told a lie. Then he asked if I'd be willing to come work for him doing odd jobs around his home. Of course I jumped at the chance. He gave me a small room of my own, decent clothes to wear and I got to eat meals with his family, with his children. He didn't send his children to the school house, he had someone come in and teach them and he had that tutor teach me to read and write, right alongside his children. To this day I do not know why I was the recipient of such generosity and mercy from that kind man, but he is the one whom you girls call Grandfather and he was the man who gave me the chance to make something of my life."

They all sat quiet around the table. Not a dry eye in sight.

Mr. Hughes continued, "I could tell Ben, you were a bit nervous coming here and meeting me today. Maybe you thought I'd look down on you because you were poor but the man who became my father taught me by example that every soul has great worth in the eyes of the Lord because every soul has great potential! I want you to remember that on this day, more than 1900 years ago, when our Lord and Savior sat in the Garden of

Gethsemane and cried unto the father for the sins of the world, that he prayed for our potential, each and every one of us. He prayed for the potential that we would repent and come unto him—and that—we must never cease doing!"

The girls could be heard sniffling and Mr. Stone wiped his eyes. Ben hung his head—Mr. Hughes was a superior man but it had nothing to do with wealth or riches, it was his love of the Lord and his fellow man which made him so. Ben knew in that moment he would work with all his might to become worthy to marry this man's daughter and become his son.

BE STILL AND KNOW THAT I AM GOD

A True Account
By Bonnie Johnson

I grew up in the suburbs and, as an adult, worked in Portland, Oregon. For nine years my office was on the 11th floor of a downtown building called the black box. I loved the bright lights, the view of Mt Hood and all the hustle. Christmas time was exciting with all the decorations and the scores of people shopping. The boats would parade on the Williamette River with an array of colored lights and music. It all gave me a sense of urgency and excitement. There were numerous cafés and coffee houses with people sitting outside in the summer. I could imagine conversations of strangers and I often met my friends for coffee to catch up on their lives.

In contrast, I relished retreats to the mountains, lakes, or beach house to soothe my harried soul. It's in those times, when all is quiet and still, when you can hear every sound, my mind wanders, forming new dreams and re-visiting old ones. When the birds sing their morning song and I sip a cup of coffee still half asleep, God's still, small voice whispers to me, "I'm in control, relax and be at peace. This is my creation made for your pleasure. I love you, you are my child." After a few days, I feel ready to go back and face new challenges.

There are times too, when I am awakened out of the deep sleep of complacency of the day to day routine and God uses circumstances to call me to His Throne. After I had moved to Colorado and was living with my brother, temporarily, I received an email from my son.

"Mom", he wrote, "My orders came through and I leave for Iraq in two weeks."
My heart fell into a bottomless pit. It felt like it was pierced by an ice pick. I felt my muscles tighten and tears welled up in my eyes. I could barely breathe and graphic pictures raced through my mind of all the war movies I had seen. "Oh Lord, please, please." I was already preparing myself for the worst. I summoned up enough strength to call my son.

"No, Mom don't come, I'll be back." He was trying to be brave for me but I could hear the concern in his voice.

"OK, I understand. The Lord will protect you and the men and women in your command. I won't be able to see you but the Lord will know where you are and He will keep you safe for me." I was trembling but kept my composure until I hung up the phone. I cried softly, so no one would hear me.

I knew why he didn't want me to come. That is a good-bye too hard for us both and he had preparation to do for his battalion and his pregnant wife. I understood. This news hit me hard. It was like a town crier running through the streets yelling, Beware, BEWARE, the enemy approaches. He was screaming with a deafening, shrill cry. There was no time to prepare. No decisions or options to weigh. I had no control nor did my son. For months, I watched every news report on TV. I went to bed and woke up to the news on the radio. I would grab the paper as soon as I got to work and read all the headlines. I searched the net for any information as to the position of his battalion. I even went so far as to get a passport in case he was taken prisoner. I was not thinking straight! It was exhausting. I couldn't seem to control myself. My brother would turn off the TV and say, "That's enough, you have to stop this!"

In the quietness of my bedroom, I'd pour out my heart to the Lord, sometimes weeping uncontrollably, sometimes very much in control. My heart ached for those who had lost their babies in combat, wondering if mine would be next. I couldn't imagine . . . .

One very special day, I was singing to myself "You are my hiding place, you always give me the songs of deliverance, whenever I feel afraid, I will trust in You." Then the Lord's still small voice encouraged me. It wasn't audible but every cell in my body received it. He said, "My child, trust me. I love your son more than you do. Whatever happens, I am in control. I will be glorified through your son's life. If his life is spared, it will be for my glory. If I choose to take him, he will be in my arms, and I will receive glory. Remember your life on earth is but a vapor. You will spend eternity with your son and loved ones who have trusted in me. You can have peace that I am watching him and I have heard your prayers. Thank you for coming to me in your despair. My peace I give you, not as the world gives, let not your heart be troubled. I want you to be joyful and confident in me."

Since that day, the peace of God has enveloped me like a soft, warm blanket. The depth of His love is beyond my comprehension. Many people, who knew of my situation, noticed a difference in me and commented on my ability to cope while my son was in harm's way. I would tell them it wasn't me but God helped me to trust Him and He gave me peace. I was afraid and very weak but God held me in His arms. God gave me the ability to function, sleep, and carry on with joy in my heart. It gave me many opportunities to witness about God's love and peace in the midst of turmoil.

My son is back in the states now (safe and healthy). His wife safely delivered their first child, a son. I am grateful for God's mercy in our lives. I have become more skilled at quieting myself, no matter what the crisis, because I know my God answers prayers and I listen for that still small voice that soothes and encourages me to love others and to know that I am loved by an awesome God.

More About Bonnie—
Bonnie Lives in Mesa, AZ with husband Don. They have 3 children and 6 grandchildren between them. Retiring soon, Bonnie plans on taking her love for writing to a new dimension. Working previously as a copywriter, she would now like to delve into articles, short stories, a memoir and eventually a novel. Having many interests in apologetics, forensics, handwriting analysis, music and sewing there is never a lack of things to do or write about.

LOOSE THREADS
By Kaine Thompson

The road looked greasy in her car headlights. Carol strained to see the yellow lines through the rain. She gripped the wheel with determination. Her dearest friend was depending on her. She glanced often in the rear view mirror, watching for blue and red lights. If they asked for her driver's license, it would be all over.

Leslie was hysterical when she called. Her kids were going to put her in a nursing home. She had fallen off the toilet and cracked her head on the sink. Her daughter found her unconscious on the floor, her panties around her ankles—dignity stripped by the body's betrayal.

She didn't blame Leslie's children. Even before the fall, her friend had not been doing well. Before, Leslie would drive every month to visit her and now here she was making the hour trip. She found no pleasure in the irony that Leslie was twenty-five years her junior.

Thunder boomed above her. She jerked and swerved back into her lane. Her hands sweated and slipped on the wheel. She checked the rear view again. They would eventually catch her; take one look at her driver's license—90—and send her home, or worse, take her license away, or her car would die and leave her stranded on the road, or

Jeremy would take away her keys, or she would shake hands with her Maker.

She sighed. She had but a few thin strands left in her tapestry. Leslie's scarlet thread was fraying and could snap any day. Too many threads cut from the loom.

They met twenty years earlier at a book club. Well-meaning friends had persuaded her to attend. She didn't want to go because intellectuals made her squeamish. She was college educated, but after forty years teaching at Lincoln Elementary she was more comfortable with young, receptive faces. She was well out of the mainstream of intellectual discourse. Her friends couldn't stop talking about the club's founder and leader, Dr. Leslie Quinlan, professor of comparative literature from Boston University.

When they entered the living room, her "friends" deposited her on a couch and disappeared. The room was full of strangers. Carol felt old. Her clothes were horribly out of date. She wanted to leave. She stood up just as Leslie came in and took a seat. Defeated, she had no choice but to sit as well.

Leslie launched into an introduction of the featured book. Everything she said opened new pathways in Carol's mind. When she finished talking, the group jumped into a discussion. The buzz from incomprehensible speech made Carol angry. She concentrated on Leslie's responses.

Carol returned the next month—alone. There was something about Leslie that excited her. She wanted to be near her, to hear her voice. Then Leslie called on her.

"Carol, you haven't shared your views. What do you think?"

"Me?"

"I'm sure you have an opinion."

"No, I don't."

She'd said it rather too angrily, so Leslie moved quickly to another and the conversation rose in a crescendo of voices. When she was at the door, Leslie waylaid her.

"I'm so sorry I put you on the spot."

"Unlike others, I don't talk nonsense just to be heard."

"Please come back. The young need to hear from the wise."

She not only came back, but the two became close friends. When Hank died, Leslie was her solace, and when Leslie went through her painful divorce, she'd been hers. Then there was that unforgettable time when Leslie had broken her leg skiing. Carol had taken care of her as if she had been her own daughter. She hadn't felt so young in years—talking long into the night, giggling on the bed, sending out for pizza and watching old movies. She could have stayed forever—but Jeremy needed her at home.

She sighed and watched for the turn-off that would take her into Phillipston. She flicked off the windshield wipers and checked the rear view. Her son had never fulfilled his potential. He could have been somebody. Instead, he worked nights as an accountant for a chain of convenience stores. He never dated and he never left home.

It was her fault. She'd made it too easy for him. He'd filled the void after Hank's death. He took out the trash and mowed the lawn. He bought groceries. Those beef ribs yesterday were not to her liking. Disgusting—him sucking on them, smacking his lips and wiping them with the back of his hand. She couldn't believe she had given birth to this gauche, developmentally arrested sixty-three-year-old man.

A car horn screamed. She hit the shoulder and struggled to regain control. She jerked the wheel and bumped back onto the slippery asphalt.

"Pay attention, Carol," she said aloud.

She must stop woolgathering—only another fifteen minutes. She kept her eyes moving by trying to identify landmarks along the way. The white fence paralleling the road was the Murphy place. Coming up around the bend would be the Perkin's house. Mary Perkin had passed away years ago. They had been at Lincoln together. She thought about Mary's kids. Matthew Perkin died in Viet Nam, Matty from breast cancer—all of them gone.

Near her turn-off, she was confronted by blue and red flashing lights. She slammed on the brake. A police officer was in the road. She didn't know what to do. Turn around? He was beckoning her forward. She prayed he wouldn't notice her shriveled face and hands. He absently waved her on as he watched his fellow officers pull open the door of a crumpled car. The colored strobe lights flickered on the unconscious driver's blood-splattered face. Red. Blue. Red. Blue.

She took her turn and left the accident behind, concentrating on the yellow stripes in the road. Was that the face of death? Was death an angel, a glowing, divine face of mercy and love? Or was it just a hideous corpse full of maggots? Perhaps death was but a flip of the switch— ON/OFF—bright day one moment and then eternal night. Her hope was in eternal life.

He looked middle-aged. What better way to go? In the strength of days, blithely driving down the road, then Wham! Better than watching the body disintegrate, with skin losing its elasticity, bones crumbling, friends leaving one by one.

Poor Leslie was a quarter century younger and fighting death off as hard as she could. She was sick all the time, then her hip, and now this. What made Leslie's clock wind down before its time and hers tick on and on?

She pulled in front of Leslie's house, slowly uncurled her legs and allowed the circulation to return before she stood up. She limped to the front door and went in. She found her friend in the bedroom and quickly covered her shock. Leslie's cheek was a hideous greenish purple. A bandage covered one eye. Her emaciated body was propped up on pillows, covered by a crocheted afghan.

"Oh, Carol. I was so worried," Leslie said, rising up to embrace her. "Where've you been?"

"There was an accident on Route 2."

"You poor dear. I've been thinking how selfish I am. It should be me seeing you."

"It was nothing. How are you?"

"Frantic. They're trying to kill me. Put me in a home. A home!"

"Nonsense. It's called assisted living; operative word *living*."

Leslie sniffed. "You make me feel ungrateful."

"What's wrong with going where you'll be taken care of? Sounds rather nice."

"Nice?" Leslie wailed, clenching the afghan in her fists. "I hate them deciding for me."

Leslie's anxiety alarmed her. There was terror on her face. Carol recalled the face of the man in the car as she listened to her friend, patting her leg through the afghan. A loose thread caught on her ring.

"You have a loose thread," she said interrupting.

"Wh-at?"

"A loose thread. If you don't do something the pattern will unravel."

"Who cares? It's too old to save."

"Doesn't mean it's not useful. Look, if I tie this red thread to the white one..." Her gnarled fingers tied off the white thread. She pulled on the red thread, tied it off and brought the two together, changing the design.

"Well, I'll be," she said. "You know, Leslie, next time it'll be me in a crumpled car."

"Don't say that."

"It's true. It's time to change the pattern."

"What are you talking about?"

"Loose threads. Us. Two loose threads."

"I'm not following..."

"Tied together we are useful—to each other. Why can't we both go?"

"Are you saying you'd go there with me?"

"I am. Call your kids and make them happy."

"But what about Jeremy?"

"He won't mind. He's not going anywhere."

More About Kaine—

Kaine Thompson began her life on the shores of Maryland but grew up on the desert plains of Idaho where the wild things roam. Writing has been a lifelong passion and has served her well as a reporter, college administrator and editor. She is the author of several books, screenplays, and short stories that celebrate and encourage women. She holds a Master's degree in writing and teaches creative writing. She currently lives in Mesa, Arizona.

Website: www.e-maginativewriting.com

Facebook: kainethompson-author

List of published works:

Remember Her For This: A Study on the Women in the Gospels (Amazon, July 2016 release)

Superstition Murder Club (Amazon, 2015)

I Remember Nobody (Smashwords, 2013)

The Living Stones (Smashwords, 2012)

FemCorps (Smashwords, 2009)

GET VERY FAR AWAY
A True Account
By Anne Marie Kensington

When Joe picked me up from work he announced, "I have a terrible headache, so we won't be able to go out with the group tonight to celebrate your birthday."

"Oh no, is it that bad?" I questioned innocently. He was driving but looked to be in pain. "I've been looking forward to seeing everyone tonight? I know Judy baked a cake. We'll have to call them and tell them we aren't coming."

A few moments of silence followed and then Joe's open hand struck my face. "Ouch!" My mind filled with questions. *What on earth was that? Why did he do that?* I didn't understand...

"Put a package of frozen peas on your cheek and it won't bruise as much," he said.

Frozen food works to ease welts and bruises? Who knew? How did he know that? Who hits people? Why is he so angry? Was all this because of a headache?

As I lay in bed that night I examined our conversation, sentence by sentence and word by word. *What did I say to make him so angry?*

Re-doing and over-doing my eye makeup the next morning, I hoped my co-workers wouldn't notice the remaining purple area around my eye. A package of frozen peas has its limits.

Did I fool everyone? Did I fool anyone? What if they asked about it? What would I say?

My life with Joe developed into a different normal in the months that followed. Small bursts of anger became typical. His explosions didn't seem all that unusual anymore, but him striking me, well—it didn't happen very often.

After one fun night out with friends, it was clear I had gone home with a monster. He slapped and slapped and slapped me some more. "If I can't have you, I'll make sure no other man wants you," Joe shouted. *Is that why he always goes for my face? What is he talking about?* I never flirted because I knew he was jealous. *Do I have enough bags of frozen vegetables in the freezer?*

The next morning my face was unrecognizable. I called work. "I am really sick with the flu and I won't be in for a few days," I said.

Deep brownish-purple turned to tannish-brown to lighter purple to greenish-yellow, before finally returning to my normal fair skin color. The bad case of the flu I claimed to have, necessarily lasted for an entire week, which gave my skin almost ten days to repair itself.

Since our laundry area was in the center of the apartment complex. Joe did the laundry for fear people would see my face. What would we say?

He threw me across the room almost as easily as he threw the lamps. My treasures were tossed and broken, but the half empty cartons of milk smashed into the linen closet made the most work for me. Everything had to be washed. Unhappily, I had very clean linens.

What am I doing that makes him so mad? He loves me. I'm sure he won't do it again. His tears prove he's sincere, don't they?

In the seven tumultuous years that followed, I left him three times. Each time his charismatic charm melted my resistance and I returned. When his big brown eyes fixed on mine, as he proclaimed his love for me, my will power turned to mush. I so much wanted a happy life with him.

The first time I went back, my daughter, Jackie was born making us a family. My pretty girl now needed a father.

Joe was home early one Friday and wanted to take Jackie to the Dairy Queen—just Daddy and Jackie. Our new baby, Jimmy, would stay home with me.

Maybe he's home early because for once he didn't stop at the bar? Wrong. He got off work early and had stopped just long enough to make him unsteady. He scooped Jackie up in his arms. They waved good-bye and headed to the car. Joe soon discovered he left his keys behind and back they came.

Maneuvering down the steps to our apartment, he stumbled and nearly dropped her. That was enough for Jackie. She lost all interest in the outing. Relieved that it didn't have to be me to cancel the DQ trip, I resumed feeding my baby. I didn't notice Joe's changing temperament; however, he had been sitting on the couch seething.

Without warning, his construction worker hands were crushing my neck strangling me.

"You have turned my kids against me!" he cried, half sobbing. With Jimmy cradled tightly in my left arm, and my right hand holding his bottle, I had no hand free with which to fight. But both hands wouldn't have helped. He was too strong.

Something, it must have been God, told me to remain calm. Jackie stood beside me. The terror I saw in her eyes let me know that if she sensed my fear, it would be her undoing.

What if he kills me? Will he also kill the kids? Could he raise the kids? No, he'll be in prison. Will the state take the kids?

Finally, for some reason unknown to me, he took his hands from my neck and hurried into the bathroom.

I ran to the phone and called the police. "My husband just tried to kill me," I said. They arrived quickly.

"He just tried to strangle me. Can you please arrest him" I begged as I opened the door to the officers. Turning around to point to the abuser, there he sat on the couch, holding Jimmy for the first time ever. Why, he almost looked like a contestant for Father of the Year! *Did he suspect*

that the knock on the door might be the police?
How did he pick up Jimmy so quickly?

Noting the visible prints on my neck from his hands, one officer said, "Ma'am we can't arrest him, but we do suggest one of you leaves until things calm down."

Now what? The officers were my only hope. I had counted on them to give us the time to escape. If they won't lock him up, will we survive?

Of course, I wouldn't leave without my babies and it was their bedtime. Joe said, "I'll leave." And he did, he went back to the bar.

As soon as he left, I called my friend Grace. She and her husband, Jake, sometimes played cards with us on Friday nights. It was normal for them to have their police scanner on so I wondered if they might have heard the domestic violence call to our address and been worried about us.

I wanted them to know that for the moment, we were okay. Also, with that call, good friends knew that the kids and I were in serious, unresolved danger.

"Call me in the morning when you have a plan. I will help you in any way I can," Grace offered.

After the kids and I were all in bed, Joe returned from the bar. Hearing his key in the door, I took a deep breath. Pretending to be asleep, I watched him as if he were an intruder. He stood for a time over Jimmy's crib, which was in our room. *What is he thinking? What is he going to do?* Smelling the booze from a few feet away, I didn't move. I listened but heard no sound from him. He climbed into bed and went to sleep.

I hardly slept. In the morning I called my sister Jan in Minnesota. Two years older, Jan had often looked after me when we were little and also had saved me more than once as an adult. Though humiliating, I needed another rescue.

She knew from the previous times when I left Joe that we were in constant danger. She couldn't know, though, that this time it had nearly been fatal. Each time I left him, Jan pleaded with me not to go back. But I always did. I covered for him again and again.

I didn't know the violent attacks would escalate with each incident. He was tragically insecure and insanely jealous. I was unsophisticated and had no idea what to do. I never knew of a woman who was abused by her husband.

While my own father was a bit controlling, he never struck my mother. He controlled the checkbook totally. She never wrote a check until their divorce, when she had to. Whether any of us kids were sick enough to be taken to the doctor, had to be my father's decision. He was controlling, but he wasn't violent towards her. He was a good father for the most part.

To be knocked around by someone who I thought loved me just didn't make sense. I had already left him three times, but always went back because I couldn't mentally or emotionally process the reality of what kept happening. I guess I didn't want to face the truth.

But everything was different now. I had two babies to protect. It didn't matter why he did what he did. I knew we were all going to die if I continued to be in denial. My self-worth was at its lowest point. I had to develop strength and courage now to save my babies. If we were going to survive, we had to get away, very far away. He had limited funds and would not be able to follow us across the country.

When I called my sister, Jan, at 8:00 AM the next morning, Saturday morning, Joe was still asleep. In a soft voice, I whispered, "Can you meet the kids and me at the airport in Minneapolis this afternoon?"

Without hesitation she answered, "Yah," even though it would take her nearly three hours to get to the Twin Cities.

"Good." I was relieved. "And I hate to ask, but can you also wire money for our tickets to the airport?"

"Yah?" She agreed with a question in her voice. I couldn't take the time to explain. I had checked the airline schedule so I could tell her what time our flight would arrive if she would pay for our tickets. She would understand everything soon enough if it all worked.

Suspecting this moment may come one day, I had been accumulating a little money, but in Joe's tirade the night before; he went through all the drawers and cupboards and snatched my stash. The only cash he didn't find was one dollar bill I had in a separate pocket in my wallet.

My friend Grace would take us to the airport. Her life could be in danger for helping us, but she was our only hope.

Because it was Saturday morning and Joe could possibly spend the morning at home and would notice me packing, I told him, "The kids and I are going to Minnesota and leaving today."

Then came the waterworks! Remorse, sorrow, contrition, and repentance, accompanied real tears that flowed. It didn't move my heart this time. I had fallen for those words too many times. I knew it wasn't true. None of it was true!

After realizing I wasn't to be persuaded this time, Joe got dressed and ready to head out for the day. "If this is really what you want," he said, "I'll come back and take you to the airport. What time does your plane leave? And by the way, don't pack any of your clothes that you bought with my money."

Hmmm, that would be a problem because recently having given birth, nothing fit me except three or four new outfits. Since I wasn't working, I guessed it was technically his money that purchased them. He didn't care about my clothes, of course, but rather hoped to put one final obstruction in front of me—one he thought would finally put an end to my hope of leaving.

Thankfully, Joe left, so I had to move quickly. Jan called to say the tickets were confirmed and waiting for us at the airport.

I called Grace. "Can you pick us up mid-morning? Our plane doesn't leave until this afternoon, but I want to be gone long before he comes to pick us up."

"Of course, I'll come now and I can help you pack," Grace offered.

I called the police station to ask if Joe could really keep me from taking my clothes. "Your clothes are yours, regardless of whose money purchased them. We can come to your apartment and be a visible presence while you pack if you think it will help," they offered.

"No, that shouldn't be necessary. He isn't home now and I expect to be gone before he comes back," I said.

The police dispatcher asked for our airline, departure time, and the flight number. I thanked him and hung up.

Joe's willingness to drive us to the airport was an offer I knew I couldn't accept. Instinct told me that if we got into the car with him, it would be the last ride any of us took. He didn't know Grace was coming to pick us up or even that I had called her. I couldn't take a cab because he had taken all my cash. Joe assumed I was out of options. We had to be gone before he returned.

Earlier I saw my upstairs neighbor in the laundry room. We were friends so I explained what was going on. She had two dollars in her pocket and insisted that I take them. That brought my walking around money up to three dollars.

Grace arrived. "Let me take your winter coats and boots home with me and ship them to you later in Minnesota," She suggested.

"Oh that's a great idea," I answered. I really needed Grace's help and was so grateful for her help.

I wondered if my heart might jump out of my chest while we packed. Grace helped me put the kids and the suitcases into her car. As we pulled away, I kept looking back fearing Joe might have returned and follow us. I wouldn't feel safe until we were in the air.

Arriving at the airport, I had two kids, three dollars, and four suitcases. One of the suitcases was filled with cloth diapers. With no money, I knew Jimmy would be using them for the duration.

Grace helped me check the luggage. I carried the diaper bag, my purse, and of course, my baby. Jackie's little fingers tightly grasped my index finger on the other hand. She knew something big was happening but didn't know what it all meant. I couldn't begin to explain it to her.

There were nearly a dozen police officers present near our airline gate at the airport. They didn't speak to me but they watched us. Maybe they had talked to Grace's husband, Jake, a former police dispatcher, or maybe they'd talked to the officers who noted the marks on my neck the night before. I never knew which it was, but seeing the officers, made me feel safer.

We boarded the plane and in a few hours we landed at the Minneapolis-St. Paul International Airport. When I spotted Jan standing at the gate, a sense of relief flowed through me. My chin quivered and tears ran.

When Jan saw my tears, she was blinking away her own. Not wanting Jackie to be more traumatized than she already had been, I fought to regain my composure. Finally, we were safe with family who would not let us go hungry or homeless. It all happened so fast. Friday evening I was being strangled and Saturday night we were hundreds of miles away in a secure place.

Wow! We had just been part of a real live miracle. So many things had to come together perfectly, in order to get us to safety, and they all did. Everything worked.

But I didn't know the whole story.

After we put the kids to bed, we finally had a chance to talk. I began to relate to Jan, and her husband, the ugly details of the night before. I explained why we desperately needed their help to escape. They were shocked to see the marks on my neck still visible more than 24 hours later.

Jan told me the reason it sounded like there was a question in her voice during our phone call. She didn't think she'd be able to find a place capable of wiring money on a Saturday morning from their rural Minnesota small town. Her only hope was the one travel agency in town.

"The phone at the agency rang several times. I worried that no one would be there," Jan said. "Finally the owner picked up the phone."

"Our agency isn't open on Saturdays," said the owner, after hearing Jan's request. "I just came in to gather some papers so I can work at home. I almost didn't pick up," he said, "but something told me to answer this phone call."

He quickly transferred the money, purchased the tickets and left them in my name at the airport. Once accomplished, he called Jan, with the confirmation. That's when she called to let me know the tickets were paid for and waiting for us. I will forever be thankful to God for bringing that man into his closed office that day, at that exact time, so he could answer Jan's call and for giving me a loving and generous sister who spent her own money to rescue my kids and me.

In a few weeks, the local school hired me for a secretarial position. We were able to move into low-income housing nearby. Our family was on our way to a new life.

A few more weeks passed and Joe's mother called. She and I had almost no history. To her I didn't exist. She was a mother who believed that a man's first wife was his only wife. She was a mother who, for a time had prayed for Joe to become a priest. When that didn't happen, she couldn't let go of her belief of only one wife. Therefore, I couldn't exist.

"This is Helen. How are you, Anne?"

"I'm fine." Did she notice the chill in my voice?

"I'm calling to tell you I'm worried about Joe. He's very depressed. He says he can't live without you. He has changed. He even went to anger management therapy. He needs you to come back."

I took a deep breath. Then I said, "If he has truly changed then that will be good for him and maybe some other woman, and by the way, you might want to welcome that woman into your life. However, I'm done. The spell is broken. Please tell him I'm not at all interested in what he needs."

Sometime later Joe called to beg me to return. But he called collect. I wouldn't accept the call. He and the operator both pleaded with me to accept.

He promised to send me twenty dollars and I promised to hang up, which is what I did.

Anne Marie Kensington

THE TINIEST TEACHER
A True Account
By Alice Klies

A maze of machines, wires, hoses and blaring alarms overwhelmed me. Nurses and doctors scurried around the room like ants building a colony. Just short of forty-five, I had delivered a one-pound nine-ounce baby girl almost three months early. I wanted to see her, hold her and count her fingers and toes. I wanted to feel her breath against my cheeks.

A nurse pushed my wheelchair close to the incubator. A handwritten sign read, 'Baby Klies'. I leaned forward while my hands clutched the arm rails on my wheelchair. My stomach churned. A weak cry escaped my lips. Tears that had pooled in the corners of my eyes started to flow freely down my flushed cheeks. "She is so tiny," I whispered.

Wires and tubes pierced all parts of my baby's minute torso. Jaundiced, her eerie-yellowed skin, against the white sheet, made me glance away. I gasped. My baby's body seemed to glow under phototherapy lights that shone bright above her. My hand clutched my chest. I reached out to grab my husband's hand.

A tiny blindfold covered my baby's eyes. I leaned closer to the incubator. Nothing about her looked real. Blue veins, which resembled roads on a map, veered in trails beneath her skin. Only eleven inches long, her bird like legs twitched. Monkey-like downy fuzz graced her limbs and torso. I longed to touch her tiny fingers that were no longer than the red sulfur tip of a wooden kitchen match.

I collapsed against the back of the wheelchair. My body swayed back and forth. The nurse put her hands on my shoulders and kneaded her fingers deep into my muscles. My head spun with questions. "What are all the wires for? What's wrong with her?"

The nurse stroked my hand. She cocked her head to one side before she answered. "A preemie's nervous system is not developed, so your baby can't shiver or sweat. Sensors need to be attached to her skin to assure us that she is neither too hot nor too cold. If this isn't monitored, she might burn up calories she can't afford to lose. Preemies are born without subcutaneous fat, which is the thermal layer directly under the skin that controls a baby's temperature."

Then, the nurse pointed to some little white patches along my baby's chest wall. "The alarm attached to her chest, monitors apnea. When your baby forgets to breathe, it is called apnea. If these spells go undetected, her heart rate can slow down. This is called Bradycardia, which can cause sudden death."

I couldn't hold my tears any longer and they began to streak down my face. "Why isn't she crying?"

"A preemie's cry can't be heard when they have a tube in their mouth. Later, when the tube comes out, your baby's throat may be so sore, that crying is too painful."

I turned my head into my husband's shoulder. Unable to contain my grief, I sobbed. My eyes pleaded with the nurse. "What am I suppose to do? Will she be all right? What happens next?"

Just then a kind of take-charge type doctor, who had been standing nearby, spoke up, "You see Alice, our staff is especially trained to do everything in their power to keep your baby alive. Once treatment for each individual child begins, there are no guarantees, only probabilities." He stopped, drew in a deep breath of air and continued, "Even babies who do well can suddenly take a turn for the worse. I sometimes think of treatment as a kind of obstacle course, we might jump one hurdle, but a bigger one might be just around the corner."

Did I really need all this negative information? I buried my head in my hands.

In spite of an only two per-cent chance of survival however, and after a three-month stay in a Neonatal Intensive Care Unit, we finally brought our little survivor home. She had more than doubled her body weight to weigh three pounds fourteen ounces when we left the hospital. Her life started in a substitute womb surrounded with bright lights and buzzing monitors. With the amazing care of all involved, she overcame all odds against her. Who knew that she was about to teach me lessons that would enrich my life beyond measure?

Lesson One: Patience
My first lesson was that a preemie baby requires patience in every aspect of their care. One

constant lesson on patience took place when the monitor attached to my little one would blare an electronic wailing sound whenever she would stop breathing. I would then quickly place my hand on her chest and gently massage it until she gulped a breath. Patience helped me remain calm during the many months she wore the monitor.

I also had to exercise patience at bath time as I would run a marathon to undress my baby girl, place her in the water, and take her back out again. Only when I would wrap her tightly in a warmed towel retrieved from the oven, would she stop screaming. I often mused. "Patience takes a deep breath. One day she will soak for hours."

Lesson Two: Perseverance

Nerve endings, not completely formed at birth, had to be stimulated. Three times a day I massaged tiny legs and arms with soothing oils and wrapped my daughter in soft fluffy towels—perseverance kept me focused.

Specialists warned how overstimulation might devastate her and cause severe meltdowns. Doctor's cautioned "Guide her gently into a loving environment, one with as little over stimulation as possible. Remember her first memories were negative ones." They reminded me that my child had traded the soft material flesh of my womb for a high-tech hospital ward subjected to unnatural manipulations. Perseverance, in spite of meltdowns, helped me find ways to sooth her.

Neonatal specialists offered further advice. "Preemies respond best to bold, contrasting colors or graphics. Music can soothe them as well." So I placed black, white and red pictures and mobiles in her crib. I bounced her, talked to her constantly, and played classical music throughout the house.

Doctor's also advised us to use soft-spoken discipline in her toddler years. In spite of family remarks that we spoiled her, perseverance taught my husband and I to stay firm to expert advice and ignore snide comments.

I placed her in a swing that I twirled in circles to stimulate her central nervous system. She had arrived too soon with vital brain wiring unfinished. A NICU can't insure that brain maturation follows its proper course. Perseverance paid off, because I witnessed dramatic results by sticking to this regimen. She walked and spoke way before any timeline that Neonatal doctors suggested she might.

I snipped tags out of her clothing. I purchased socks without seams. If tags remained, she would scream and wrestle out of clothing or pull socks with seams from her feet. Trips to the doctor for general shots or exams created drama comparable to a Frankenstein movie. Perseverance gave me insight to find clothes without tags, seamless socks and purchase a white jacket to encourage doctor games to lessen her fears.

Lesson Three: Acceptance

My motto became "It is what it is." Extreme cold or hot temperatures put my tiny girl into a tailspin. She could wade in a 90-degree pool and with an outside temperature of 115 degrees, (Arizona summers) her lips would turn blue and she shivered for ten minutes. In winter, her tiny hands turned blue even with gloves. Acceptance let me "get over it." She never outgrew this.

We lived in an area of new construction. She hollered at the top of her lungs every time she saw a tractor. We had no idea why she did this, but the construction went on for months, therefore so did the outbursts. Acceptance nudged me to take alternate routes to avoid tractors.

When it was time to remove the heart monitor, I freaked out. The monitor was like one of her body parts. Every time she stopped breathing it blared. I knew I'd feel naked without the security of its constant guardianship. The first four evenings without the monitor, I sat by the crib and watched the rise and fall of her chest. Acceptance convinced me to put my trust in the Lord and go to bed.

She had a life threatening experience from an allergic reaction to penicillin. For three days I held her and slathered her body with ointments to sooth the pain and itch of hives that covered her with grapefruit size welts. Constant ear infections caused numerous broken eardrums and her fragile lungs—susceptible to bronchitis and asthma—threatened to put her back in the hospital many times. Acceptance helped me realize that health problems might be her norm.

Lesson Four: Humor
She woke every night with sleep terrors. This continued into her teen years. When she was little I managed to get her back to sleep by curling up beside her. I tucked her safely in my arms and

rubbed her back. One night, at age five, I rushed to her side.

"Honey, you don't have to be scared. God is here with you. He will keep you safe."

"Is He in my closet?"

I snuggled closer to her. "I suppose He is."

She bolted upright, jumped out of bed and ran to the closet. She slid the closet door open.

"Get outta my closet God. You can't help me if you're locked in there!"

She ran back to the safety of my arms, pulled the covers over her head and shivered back into a slumber. My shoulders slumped. I sighed. Humor helped me cope.

Intellectually, I knew my daughter was unique. Nonetheless, I struggled with the fact that I compared her progress to other children. I often told our friends. "I think one of the most common fears I have is will my baby be normal?"

At age six, she looked at me, screwed up her little nose so that a bunch of wrinkles formed on its side and said, "Why do you worry so much about me mommy? God put me here for a reason!"

My stomach tightened with guilt, then I laughed. "I'm sure you're right." Humor brought laughter and solace.

Lesson Five: Compassion

I always thought I was a compassionate woman, that is, until I watched the faces of people when she would become unglued in any public place— when she would display actions that didn't appear 'normal.' I realized that the dropped jaws that spouted 'tsk, tsk,' mirrored my own reactions before her birth. My compassion was more like pity when I saw any disabilities or unusual behavior. I realized that I felt pity for all that the person wasn't, instead of seeing them for all that they actually were. Shame bubbled through my heart. I found out that compassion is honest, sympathy and acceptance.

Lesson Six: Tolerance

When my little girl's outbursts caused family to make snide remarks about my parenting, I wanted to withdraw into a cocoon or lash out at them. I had a special child that I expected people to be tolerant of, yet, my own lack of tolerance when people made their remarks—I realized with guilt—put me in the same category of intolerance. After all, wasn't I being intolerant of their intolerance? I learned to remain silent, breathe and accept. True tolerance accepts without judgment.

Lesson Seven: Prejudice & Minority

I came from a middle class, white background and I never really understood what it might feel like to be a minority, although I frequently felt compassion or sorrow for other who experienced prejudice. I started to understand how minorities might feel a little more deeply however, after I gave birth to a preemie that displayed unusual behavior throughout her childhood and into adulthood, because I became a type of minority— experiencing prejudice via my child. My apathy strengthened in this area. Now, my call to the world is "Prejudices are evil in today's world."

Lesson Eight: Importance of Research

Every three months during my baby's first year, a specialist evaluated her. Each visit, I came away with advice to help in her advancement. Doctor's warned me that I might have to cope with a strong willed, frustrated child who would develop differently. They cautioned that developmental milestones of preemies don't occur at the ages listed in child development books. Research helped me understand what might lie ahead.

Social skills tormented her. She didn't make friends easily. She complained frequently that no one liked her. The research that I did, clarified that pre-term children, especially females, can be demanding and bossy and often have fewer friends.

The most noticeable disability she struggled with was math skills. I counseled with teachers and psychologists constantly. I used every skill suggested to help her. I purchased musical math CD's, taped numbers on walls and mirrors, traced problems on her back and hired tutors. Once again my research proved that one-third of babies born pre-term, especially under three pounds, require school services by second grade—most often in math. I found that there is an actual name given, called dyscalculia, where studies show there is often less grey matter (brain cells) or less brain activity in the specific area of the brain known to process mathematics.

At the age of twelve, doctor's diagnosed her with Panic Disorder. I read more research that showed it was common in pre-term babies who weighed less than three pounds. Symptoms of anxiety and depression were noted in 9 out of 12 preemies that were studied.

She had exaggerated fears. She wouldn't ride a bicycle, use a playground swing, climb, or go down a slide like most children. Research reports that pre-term babies are less coordinated, which may be related to brain development and effects of neonatal intensive care. Research helped me understand my preemie.

I don't have a certificate that hangs on a wall to prove the lessons I learned from my preemie baby girl. But, I know I learned valuable lessons and so I hope that my attitude and actions speak volumes of change to our friends, family and strangers I interact with.

I no longer tap my toe in frustration. I know God is laughing at that one. I really do value patience. I've found that if I can't make something work, I persevere with a vengeance to find solutions. I work hard to accept trials as they crop up. I try to seek humor and blessing in every ugly situation I encounter. I think I am more compassionate to minorities and to those who are less fortunate. I've started to volunteer with special needs organizations and I try to be tolerant of most circumstances, even of that driver who cuts in front of me... fewer cuss words... really, I mean it! I work hard every day to forget and forgive the small stuff. Oh, and even though I hate the computer, I actually

Google research when I don't understand something.

      Now an adult—My little girl—who isn't so little any more, dances to her own drum but I love the beat she dances to. I never expected that teachers could come in such tiny packages? I am, however, eternally grateful that I learned so much from my one pound preemie.

More About Alice—

Alice is president of Northern Arizona Word Weaver's, which is a chapter of Word Weavers International, Inc. Word Weavers exists to educate, train, and support writers who desire to promote a biblically based Christian worldview. Alice is currently writing a memoir. She can be reached at alice.klies@gmail.com. She hopes her essays will encourage and bring a smile to a weary heart. Alice is published in eight anthologies, five Chicken Soup For The Soul books, Angels on Earth, WordSmith Journal and AARP.

KISSED BY KAYA
A True Account
By Liz Hufford

When my brother-in-law Reverend Bill's mission took him to Canada, he knew his youngest child Rob would delight in hockey and skiing. At that time Rob was not old enough for Bill to think about French girls. But years later Rob married his beautiful Quebecer Penny.

The couple moved to Vermont after the birth of their son Chad. Rob worked at a ski lodge. Canada had had its influence.

Four daughters joined the family. Yet as 2012 arrived, the parents were forced to consider an emptying nest. In the fall Chad would be a high school senior; Brooke, the eldest daughter, was about to get her driver's permit. Then came the surprise--a sixth child! Rob announced the pregnancy on Facebook, posting an old wedding day pic of he and his bride playing hockey in tux and gown. The caption read "19 year veteran, shoots, scores to make it 6-0."

The couple learned early that this would be a Down syndrome baby. The doctor assured Penny that the pregnancy could be terminated promptly. I sometimes try to imagine his reaction to her furious response. She and Rob believed any child of God was "fearfully and wonderfully made." She would carry her baby to term.

In September 2012, Kaya was born. Rob's first response to his fifth daughter was "she's beautiful." True, she was perfect on the outside, but the parents soon learned that she had heart and breathing problems. Subsequently doctors discovered her digestive system was incomplete. She lacked an anus. Operations, breathing apparatus, at-home nurses, and close calls followed. Through it all Kaya persevered.

I am not sure how my nephew and his wife landed on her name, but I am touched by its appropriateness. On the Hopi reservation, the name means "my elder little sister," an old soul, wise beyond years. In Indonesia it means "wealthy," in Quechan "tomorrow."

"Elder little sister" may seem ironic, but Kaya is our wise one. She lives in the moment, sitting on the floor in a sunbeam, one armed looped around her dog. "Be still and know that I am God." Kaya's wealth is not the cool, hard gold of Midas. She is embraced in the warm arms of those who love and care for her. When she was an infant, her brother carried her like a football. No wonder he seldom fumbled on the field! The previous baby of the family, Kami, could clear a trach tube before she entered first grade. "Anyone who does not provide for their relatives, and especially for their own household, has denied the faith." As for tomorrow, it is an uncertainty for Kaya, as it is for all of us. Even the Lord's Prayer emphasizes only "give us this day." Where Kaya is concerned we "take therefore no thought for the morrow."

So far Kaya has experienced three years of tomorrows. It has been a time of intermittent miracles. Her heart healed itself. An operation reconstructed her digestive system so she no longer needed a colostomy. The first dirty diaper was cause for celebration! Breathing problems have lessened, but a typical childhood illness can land her in the hospital. Still, being partially free from tubes and machines has resulted in improved mobility. She has taken her first steps, stopping between them to give herself a round of applause. Because of a life-saving tracheostomy, Kaya doesn't speak. She does sign, even to the dog. "Sit!" Kaya signs, and Ivy obeys. Unless Kaya's trachea grows and firms (or doctors construct one), she cannot talk and breathing problems continue to jeopardize her life.

But you wouldn't know it to see her skiing and sledding with a little help from her friends. When health permits, she attends pre-school. When illness keeps her home, she snuggles with Ivy, her therapy pup, provided by Make-a-Wish. Even when Kaya's ailing, she still plays and eats with gusto.

Not everyone would make the same decision as Penny and Rob. It may not always be the right choice. But I have been proud of their commitment and amazed by what has transpired. Once when

Kaya had died and been revived, I cried for her. Then I got thinking about quality of life rather than length. How bad would it be to have known only love in your lifetime, not disappointment or betrayal or embarrassment?

A small life can have huge implications. A number of her siblings, cousins, and friends plan careers in medicine. And then there's me.

I was never at ease with those with Down syndrome. I'd put on what I hoped was an accepting smile, but I wouldn't make much eye contact for fear they'd think I was staring. That changed with Kaya. I now feel compelled to engage. Recently I met a small special needs class in the drugstore. Their teacher was doing a splendid job of teaching basic math and comparison-shopping during this field trip. One boy sported a Steelers' jacket. "Steelers 38-35," I said referring to a recent game. We high-fived. Eyes lit up, and I heard rustling as clothing was unbuttoned or unzipped. The other students had a Steeler tee shirt or scarf. I had discovered a gaggle of fans. A discussion ensued on favorite players. I'm afraid I disrupted the teacher's lesson, but maybe it just changed. We all learned a bit about how humans interact.

I would bet money that Kaya is the most photographed sixth child in the history of the world. On Facebook the extended family has watched her firsts—verbalization, teetering steps, day at school. This July, at a family reunion, everyone will get to meet her. To me the event will be anticlimactic. I have already been kissed by Kaya.

More About Liz—

Liz Hufford was raised in Pennsylvania but has lived in Arizona long enough to attain faux-native status. She is the published author of poems, articles, essays, and short stories. Her work has appeared in THE BINNACLE, DASH, 300 DAYS OF SUN, TALES FROM THE COURTROOM, and THE MAGAZINE OF FANTASY AND SCIENCE FICTION, among others. She writes when it's too hot to be outside in the garden. POEMS SHORT STORIES NONFICTION
Eastern Standard Summer No Man War Story
Living with Scorpions Speed Dating Gone Accourting
Rider Remorse Tablets of Stone Rattlesnakes & Rapists
Koan on Aging The Book Learners Gold for Grabs Metaphysician This Offer Expires Drawing the Lines

THE HUNT

A True Account
By Dianna Beamis Good

Darkness surrounded me. My eyes crept over the top of the warm blankets and my nose instantly inhaled the frigid air of the early morning.

"Are you sure you want to do this?" My dad whispered and glanced at my two sisters still asleep in their beds.

I nodded and slipped out of the cozy covers and dressed in the warmest clothes I owned. I tiptoed down the dimly lit stairwell which led to the main floor of my grandparents' home. The house thrilled me with its small secret cupboards and corridors. At times it transformed into a castle with a lone tower where dragons lay in wait, a ship with pirates and a huge cave with trolls to battle. A house of mystery and fantasy where I could lose myself for hours— magical to a seven year old girl.

After I made my way down the dark staircase, I heard hushed voices from my grandmother's modest kitchen. I slowly stepped in and immediately felt shy and very small. I wanted to run back to the warmth and security of my bed.

The men held their mugs to their chest and discussed the morning activities. I paused at the open door and peeked in to see them as they sat around the wooden table in the middle of the room.

I started to turn, but my grandpa's words stopped me. "Well, good morning, little one. So are you ready to start your adventure?"

"I... I guess so." I realized my reply didn't sound very confident, so I tried again. "Yes, I am, Grandpa! How about you?"

He just looked at me and smiled, dressed in his bib overalls as always. I saw the other two men look down at me nodding their heads in appreciation of my courage. I noticed my Uncle Don first, tall, thin and quiet. I loved his smile. It made me feel like we shared a secret. My dad stood next to him. He was the reason I would get up at the crack of dawn and freeze.

A strong, handsome man, I always felt safe with him near. I never liked it when he went anywhere by himself and always jumped with enthusiasm to go with him.

Dad leaned back in his chair. "So are you ready for this? It's going to be cold and I don't want you to lag behind."

"Oh, I won't," I promised. I knew I would keep up with them no matter what. Even if I thought my feet would fall off.

We drove down the only main road and the town lay quiet. After only a couple of minutes we came to what signaled the end—the railroad tracks.

A small community made up of retired farmers and ranchers populated the area. With only a couple hundred people in the whole community, everyone always knew when all my cousins got together. We would explore the small drug store and be treated by our grandpa with stale candy or gum, but it didn't matter. This was Fall River, Kansas and I loved it.

I began to rethink my initial thoughts of hunting after I stepped out of the warmth of my uncle's truck. The icy chill of the Kansas wind penetrated my clothes and I immediately began to shiver. *How am I going to do this?*

We started to walk down the slippery tracks. I didn't know what to expect since I had never been on a quail hunt. It didn't take long for me to find out.

In the next few minutes a long bush seemed to come to life. Branches moved in opposition to the wind and several birds awkwardly tried to fly out of the brush.

"Yep, the quail are definitely around. We'll need to keep a look out," my dad roared as the wind howled.

We walked down the tracks for several minutes when suddenly, several quail flew up out of the brush. Instinctively I ducked as the reverberating shots rang out. My dad and uncle ran to pick up their quail.

"Wow, dad you got one!"

"Yep, I don't know if it was a good shot or I just got lucky, but no matter, here it is."

"What are you going to do with it now?" I admired the small quail in his hand.

"Well, if you think you can handle it, I'll show you."

"Sure, I can handle it." I fought to keep my voice steady. Actually, I didn't know what he would do, but I would handle it no matter what.

I watched intently with eyes glued to his every movement. First he took the quail by the head and to my bewilderment swung it in a circle like a lasso. My mind screamed "Stop." Fortunately no words accompanied the thought. Finally I sighed. *Well at least that's over.*

Or at least I thought, but then the worst of it came, dad took the dead bird and placed its head across the railroad tracks. My world shifted into slow motion. He placed his boot on the limp head and held the body in his right hand. Before I could think, he twisted the body and separated it from the head. Then he calmly placed the body in his pouch.

I couldn't move. I couldn't speak. My mind spun. I just stared at the small head on the ground with my mouth agape. *What just happened?* I looked around to see if my uncle or grandpa saw what my dad just did, but to my astonishment I realized they were putting small bodies into their pouches, too.

"Are you okay, Dianna? Dianna, can you hear me?" My dad's voice sounded far away.

I painstakingly pulled my gaze from the small head. Dad looked at me.

"What?"

"Are you okay?"

"Oh, yes, umm, yes I'm fine." I turned to away and tried to fight back the tears. "Yes, I'm good."

I heard the hesitation in my dad's voice as he replied, "Ok, then let's go back to the house. It's getting colder out here."

We silently made our way back to the truck, loaded up and headed back to grandpa's house.

Later I sat in my grandma's kitchen and drank hot chocolate replaying the scene over and over in my head. It all seemed so cruel and heartless. *How could he do that to such a pretty bird? Why did he have to ring its head off like that?* My thoughts went from sadness to feeling guilty about thinking badly about anything my dad did. Then I remembered the night before as we planned the trip and my dad talked about hunting. He said something about how it wasn't about the quail, but time spent with family. I hadn't really thought about it much at the time. I just wanted to go and do something really fun with my dad. *It was fun. It was an adventure, wasn't it?*

I smiled and realized I felt fine. Yes, it shocked and surprised me, but I survived. I suddenly took notice of all the activity around me. The most wonderful aroma of something like chicken filled the room. My mom and grandma walked bowls of food to the dining room. I heard my stomach growl. I stood and walked into the dining room. Everyone sat around the table.

"There you are. We were just taking about you." Dad smiled.

"Really, about me?"

"Yep, your grandpa and Uncle Don were just saying what a good job you did on your first hunting trip."

Just then my grandma brought in a huge platter with several small baked quail. It smelled delicious.

"The fruits of our hard work and you were part of it." My dad turned and looked at the meal.

I looked at the small baked quail in front of me. I felt a tinge of pride at my dad's words. I hadn't thought about the food the hunt provided. A new realization of the day's events came into focus. The shock of the morning's experiences began to fade and a new appreciation began to emerge. I knew hunting would probably not be in my future, but I became part of something bigger. The gratitude of a job well done and the memories it provided meant the most to me.

With a satisfied smile, I settled in to enjoy the meal with the rest of my family.

I have never forgotten that experience of my first hunting trip with my dad almost fifty years ago. I never knew for sure if my dad saw the tears that day, but he never spoke of them if he did. We would often reminisce of our experience and it formed a special bond between us for the rest of his life.

More About Dianna—

Dianna is a retired English teacher of 25 years. She has been journaling and writing stories for years mostly for her own enjoyment of reliving and discovering life. She is a member of the Northern Arizona Chapter of Word Weavers International and has appreciated the talent of those around her. Dianna is a wife of 37 years, mother of two and grandmother of four. She is published in two of Yvonne Lehman's anthologies *Spoken Moments* and *Stupid Moments*. Dianna has also been published in Little Cab Press *2015 Christmas Story Collection* and she hopes to get her devotional published soon.

THE GOAT AND I
A true story from the 2015 Valley Fire
By Joshua Good

Where to begin, well if you thought this story was going to be about some heroic acts of valor by myself and fellow firefighters during the Valley fire in California then I fear you might be in for a little disappointment. For you see this story is about a goat, yes a goat, not a talking goat, or a goat with magical powers, or a goat that could fly, just an ordinary goat, who went through an extraordinary ordeal.

Now just a little back story to get you caught up. I am a firefighter in Arizona, and in the late summer of 2015 I along with three of my fellow firefighters were deployed to California to help fight the blaze burning through the town of Middle Town. It was a day and a half drive for us to get there, while we traveled every news report, Facebook update, and Twitter post made us all sit up a little straighter and lean in to hear any news. The newly named Valley Fire had destroyed about

500 homes and many more were in its path. To the crew this meant that there would be no shortage of work for us when we got to the incident command post.

"Well we'd better try and get some sleep tonight," said Jon, my engine boss. "I wouldn't be surprised if they just put us straight to work when we get there."

"You don't think they'll make us go through the check in?" I asked glancing over at him.

"Nope, I bet we skip all that stuff and go straight to the fire."

I tossed and turned most of night, somehow I managed to drift off and find some rest. The next morning we got up early and drove the rest of the way to the incident command post to be given our assignment. The Operations branch explained that we were headed to Middle Town where we would meet our division supervisor who would give us more details. Time to fight some fire, or so we thought.

The drive into Middle Town made me feel I had been transported into a scene out of a strange post-apocalyptic sci-fi movie, and the closer we got the stranger it became. Few cars were on the road as we got closer and the vehicles we did see were either other fire engines or abandoned and burned. I looked out the truck window and saw power poles burned on the ground or suspended in midair by the wires used to pulse electricity to the town. They looked like strange puppets hung from cables, I half expected them to dance as much as fall down. Some of the poles were still burned and smoke curled off the tips of them like a cigar that had been discarded by some giant as he passed through. Smoke hung low in the valleys we drove past. The sun cast an eerie orange-colored glow over everything around us. We arrived in the heart of Middle Town. The devastation was worse.

We were sent to an area about four or five blocks long completely destroyed by the fire. Very few houses were upright; most were leveled to the ground. My job was to search through the rubble and look for victims, not exactly what I thought I would be doing, but it was important none the less.

My crew and I sifted through the remains of people's lives, their dishes, books, clothes, and pictures had all now been turned in to a white ash which had the consistency of powered chalk. The smell was hard to describe, if you've ever had a house fire or been near one then you would know it. A very unique, and strong mix of wood with the acrid sting of melted wires, a hint of garbage and plastic all rolled into one smell, it was everywhere.

The next day we were to patrol a different part of town called St. Helena. Some of the homes on St. Helena had survived the fire many had not. I began to sift through rubble to look for victims and extinguish any hot spots. We checked the first few houses, fortunately not finding much, except for a few chickens in their coop, a couple of excited pigs and one very unfriendly steer. I noticed a house on a burned hill.

"Hey guys let's go check that house up there on that hill. It looks like the fire made a run up through the property," I yelled. The crew and I reached the house and saw not one house, but two.

"Jon, would you look at that, how can one house be completely burned to the ground and the other not even be singed?" I stared at what use to be a family's home.

"I don't know, it could be a wind shift or different types of topography, and sometimes there is just no explanation for it."

All the trees around the destroyed house were burned and I could see the path that the fire had taken. It went all the way from the bottom of the hill up into the tree line above the two lots. I stood on what used to be the porch. I looked below into a wide burned out area. I saw something move.

"Hey did you guys see that?"

No one answered. I watched intensely to see it again. I stood and starred into the burned out forest below me. I saw a small face poke its head out from around a tree.

"Hey guys, there's something alive down there."

"What is it?" Jon asked looking down the hill.

"I don't know. I'm going to go check it out."

Jon gave me a nod. "Okay, just be careful. The last thing I need is for you to get hurt or lost out here."

"Thanks, mom, I will I promise." I yelled sarcastically back to Jon, he laughed and I headed down the hill to where I had seen the face.

As I got closer to where I had seen the movement, I slowed my pace a bit and became more attune to my surroundings. I listened, the breeze moved through the trees above me. The ground was wet and soft under my boots. I could smell a mix of pine needles and what smelled like a wet dog. Off to my side I caught a faint movement from behind a fallen tree. This must be the thing I saw when I was on the hill. What is it, a bear, or a bob cat, or maybe a deer? I inched closer excited about the cool and exotic animal that lurked in this dark burned out patch of forest. It wasn't, however, any of those cool picture or story worthy animal encounters. It was... a goat. It was a grey haired, long horned that curled off its head and almost touched it's back, goat.

"Hey! I found that thing that I saw. It was a goat."

"A what?" Jon looked down at me.

"A goat—like an eats grass and butts stuff with its head—goat."

"Really?" I could tell Jon was skeptical.

"Yea, you guys have got to come check this out."

"How could this animal have survived the fire?" They all seemed to say at once.

I walked down closer to the fence. To my surprise, the goat became interested and walked towards me. Once I got to the fence line, she, I determined that she was a girl goat, got excited and trotted up to where I was. I put my hand over the fence and she immediately pushed her head up so I could pet her. I scratched behind her ears and gave her a quick once over to see if she had been injured. I could see small black marks on her hooves where it looked like she had run through fire, her hair didn't look burned and she acted pain free. Her hair was wet from the rain the night before. It felt coarse but not unpleasant to touch. Her ears were soft and floppy and were her favorite things to have pet. An aroma of wet hay and smoke came off of her coat, which was different but not bad. How did you make it out of this? Why aren't you hurt? She tilted her head up at me with a sweet and simple expression on her face and waited for me to scratch behind her ears again.

I looked at her and pondered what she must have gone through. It reminded me of a passage in Psalm 50 verse 9, 10, and 11: *"I will not accept a bull from your household or male goats from your pens, for every animal in the forest is Mine, the cattle on a thousand hills. I know every bird of the mountains, and the creatures of the fields are Mine."* There was no explanation for this goat's miraculous survival other than the path God had for her. He made a way for this simple sweet creature to make it out of a terrible ordeal, and all she had to do was follow it. God cared enough for this goat to make it possible for her to survive. How many times has He done this for me and how many times have I missed it and wound up burned?

God sees our situations, and no matter how dire they may look to us, He has provided a way for us to survive. We just need to trust that God has not forsaken us, and He is with us in each situation. We need to be willing to look for our way out, or our place of protection God has provided us. Just like He did for my friend, the Goat.

More About Joshua—

Joshua Good lives in a small town in north central Arizona. He lives with his wife, two children, Wyatt and Katie, two cats, and his two dogs. Joshua works as a fulltime firefighter, and on his days off enjoys taking his kids on hikes around where they live. He spent 5 years in the United States Marine Corps right out of high school where he was deployed twice out of the country. Joshua loves his family and he loves his God being a member of a church almost his entire life.

THE TRIKE RIDE
A True Account
By Burton Voss

Her hair was bright—beyond pale: the color of snowy ice crystals. She knew of snow and seasonally saw it on the Hualapai Mountains to the east; but odds are she never played in any during her lifetime of five years in Kingman, Arizona. Her home in the sparsely settled Hilltop area was high desert country where kids prayed, usually in vain, for snow at Christmas.

Another house baked in the dry sun two hundred yards away. Other than that, acres of dirt, Spanish daggers, and greasewoods surrounded them. Most roads were dirt then in 1949, and a narrow one twisted around and over caliche outcroppings to provide access to both properties.

Although ageless desert was her world, a few shrubs and trees grew in her yard, planted by her grandfather. He was gone now, leaving her mom their sole support, her live-in grandmother the housekeeper and her companion. Expendable income was scarce for toys, but she played with chuckwallas and her dog, Whiskers, in the rocks overlooking the railroad cut in the hill behind the El Trovatore restaurant and motel.

Her name was Frances, a shy girl: social skills unsure and untested due to isolation. In the company of others, she was reserved and quiet, regarded as polite since she sat still and didn't draw attention to herself. Her demeanor was endearing to her mother's co-workers, the Mohave County General Hospital kitchen staff. She was also a favorite target of a cigar chomping garage owner who couldn't resist teasing a kid who dreaded the attention.

Shyness didn't dull her optimism and joy of holidays and birthdays, or any cause for celebration. She anticipated with childlike zeal the promise of presents, Easter eggs, Halloween candy, or any gifts of the particular season. However, to cause squeal-worthy excitement required a toy, a very special one, unexpected and arriving for no reason at all other than to say she was remembered.

It was a tricycle.

Used, sure, but it was red and it had handle grips, and, Oh, My! a handlebar bell. Frances now owned a big girl's tricycle, no more little wooden trike with a bench seat for her. The toddler trike became the conveyance of stuffed animals.

Frances wasted no time going places. The red trike took her everywhere at the speed of thought with the alarm bell sounding her passage. In one imagination, she was flying down the road, careening around corners in a police car, ringing her bell to warn lizards out of the way. In another, perhaps she was sounding the alarm from her fire truck on the way to save people in a burning building. Or maybe the bell was the vibrating air horn of a Greyhound bus as she nudged the behemoth into the station. Tire tracks in the dirt crisscrossed her yard as she sped from one adventure to another. What could be better? It was almost too much happiness for one small body to contain. Fortunately, she didn't have to.

A family had moved in the nearest house and they had two daughters, the youngest a whole head taller than petite Frances but near her age. She would make a friend and share all this fun.

Frances undertook the ride to her neighbors, pedaling where she could, pushing and pulling the trike around deep ruts, potholes and rock obstacles in the unmaintained road; a tough journey for a little girl with a metal vehicle half her size.

The joy was worth it as she and her friend piled on her new toy and took turns steering. They laughed, rang the bell and enjoyed playtime ... until the girl's father stormed out of the house, slamming the screen door behind him.

Red-faced he screamed at his daughter to get away from Frances. His lips contorted to spit hurtful, abhorrent words. He pointed at Frances calling her a brat, using vile swear words as adjectives. He shrieked for her to get off his property and never come back—never get near his girls again. Expletives ripping from the depth of his hatred trailed one after another to wind around her, like an evil serpent coiling her tiny chest, squeezing her breath away.

What had she done? Terrified, Frances tearfully apologized even though she didn't know why. This man told her in the most poisonous language imaginable that she was a pariah, a reject, something to exile from normal society. If it had been a movie, a champion would have shown up, punched the man in the nose, taken Frances for ice cream and everything would have been made right ... big smiles, end of story. That didn't happen.

Her apologies infuriated him and increased his abuse volume. She wanted to curl up and hide ... escape. His acidic words saturated her, eating away her person. According to him, she was nobody, deserving nothing, a crying parasite he didn't want around as if she were a contagious pox.

Under such an assault all she could do was keep apologizing. "I'm sorry. I didn't mean to ..." All she ever wanted to do was share her greatest joy and make a friend. Now the lop-sided incident flayed her until she couldn't see her home—and safety—through her tears, it might as well been over the horizon.

How does a beat-up five-year-old, struggling to walk, get home without breathing for sobbing uncontrollably while pushing a toy turned torture device? She did, though. She reached her place of unconditional love and acceptance.

Why did the man assail her? Perhaps someone has an explanation. Maybe the fact that he bought his two daughters shiny new bicycles shortly thereafter is telling. The girls never told Frances, so she never found the reason. Six decades later, Frances recalls the unexpected encounter of sharing her red tricycle with the handlebar bell. Some would reason that she might fear strangers.

The venom of the serpent's words stung her and she cried, but she wasn't infected. She never turned from the person she was then, a joyful person who wants to share her good fortune and have *you* for her friend.

More About Burton—

Burton Voss is retired in Sun City West, Arizona. He is a member of American Christian Fiction Writers, and Christian Writers of the West. He is honing the writing craft through a critique group sponsored by Gifts To Go in Surprise, AZ, ACFW, CWOW, and the writer's group sponsored by the Sun City West library. He has a historical fiction on the shelf waiting for a rewrite, and is currently writing speculative fiction.

THE HUALPAI
By Roy Voss

The rusty old Ford pickup with a cracked windshield coughed its way into the tribal police parking lot in Peach Springs, Arizona. The engine turned over several times after the ignition shut off, the diesel effect from a red-hot carbon buildup causing gasoline vapors to explode.

The driver's door swung open, and a faded denim-clad leg slowly dropped out. Then another. With an effort, the driver finally materialized beside the truck. The slightly stooped and bow-legged old Hualapai Indian ambled through the hot September sun toward the station house. He wore a battered Levi jacket in spite of the heat.

Tribal Police Chief Benjamin Grounds heard the pickup arrive, and a faint smile curled the corners of his lips. The former Army Special Forces sergeant picked up his cane and went to meet his old friend. Herman Cruz was his role model and mentor. The things he had taught Ben Grounds greased the skids for the rigorous training he endured to become a Green Beret before the wounded leg and hip that ended his military career.

"What brings you out of the trees?" Ben asked as Herman Cruz limped toward the door.

"Certainly not the paint thinner you call coffee," Cruz replied. "You have any?"

"Yep. Come into my office and I'll pour you a cup. Still want more cream and sugar than coffee?"

"That's what makes it tolerable."

Cruz went to Grounds' office while the police chief poured two cups of the freshly brewed coffee. The old man had barely made it to his chair when Grounds returned and took his seat at his desk. He knew Cruz had driven his smoky old truck the ten miles to the police station because he had something on his mind. They sipped in silence, Grounds waiting for the explanation to come out. Herman Cruz was thrifty with words, and small talk was out of the question.

After a couple of minutes, the old fellow said, "The rains have been good. There is lots of water."

"Yes. The cattle are fat and happy."

"All the springs are full. There is water in the tanques."

Ben Grounds knew this lead to something but couldn't see what.

"There is plenty of grass."

Ben just nodded and waited.

"Are you ready to make good on your promise?" Cruz asked.

Ben frowned and wracked his brain but couldn't come up with what his old friend might mean. They sat in silence while Cruz blew on his coffee and sipped.

Finally, Ben shook his head and spoke. "I'm sorry, Herman. I don't remember what promise I made you."

The old man nodded. "I thought as much. You were young. Maybe six years. You promised that when the time came, you would go with me to learn the resting places of our dead chiefs. You know. To make sure they are undisturbed. The time has come."

Ben's brain did flips. He did remember. He even remembered how excited he was at the prospect, but that was twenty-nine years ago, and things change. Now he understood all the talk about the water and grass.

Herman Cruz stared at him with unblinking eyes. Ben couldn't look away. They stayed locked in eye contact for what seemed several long minutes. Finally, Ben blew out a deep breath. "A promise is a promise. When you are ready, so am I."

"Well, I am finished training the horses for this year. No more work now, and it is time to see to this thing. I will start preparing tomorrow. We should leave the day after."

"That's pretty damn soon, Herman. Let me make sure I can get off work."

"You can get off work. Tell the council what you want to do. They will handle it."

This ended the conversation. The old Hualapai stood, thanked Ben for the coffee and wobbled his way toward the door.

"Do you want me to drive you home?" Ben asked.

Herman Cruz turned and smiled. His wrinkled face resembled the color of a piñon seed, and his teeth were stained brown and yellow. Ben loved him. "Are you speaking ill of my ride?"

"There isn't much left to speak ill of, I'm afraid."

Cruz took Ben by complete surprise. He pulled a cell phone out of the Levi jacket pocket. His smile widened. "I may be old, but I have lots of grandchildren. They are good to me. I even know how to work this thing." He gave Ben the number. "I'll call you if I don't make it home."

Old or not, Herman Cruz was still the best horse trainer on the Hualapai Reservation— maybe all of Northern Arizona. With all the summer work behind him, he now had time to train his own colts. When Ben Grounds arrived at the Cruz place, he found the old fellow already had a packsaddle on one three-year-old gelding and a saddle on another.

Ben got out of his pickup and inhaled a deep breath of the juniper-scented air. The only blemish in the cornflower blue sky was a vapor trail from a jet going toward California.

"Bring your saddle," Cruz said. "I think you will like this gray. He used to belong to a girl in Seligman. She spoiled him so bad he became nearly useless. Her father brought him here so I could fix him, but never came back. Someone told me they moved away." Cruz laughed. "I think the guy was glad to get rid of this horse. His mistake."

It took another hour to finish loading the packs before they were ready to mount up and ride off. Ben led an extra saddle horse, and Cruz led the pack animal.

"I don't know if you understand how significant this journey is, Ben. The bones of these old chiefs are important to us. At least us old guys.

These are sacred places, and we don't want them to be disturbed."

"I think I understand, Herman. I will be happy to carry on this tradition, one day."

He understood more than Herman knew. For the last two days, he had occupied most of his free time talking to elders and reading about his people's culture. It amazed him how far he had departed from his heritage and was anxious to learn how Cruz would deal with the ghost problem. Ben knew that most of the tribe, especially the older people, did not like to be anywhere near where someone had died.

Cruz set his young gelding off at a fast walk that would cover about five miles per hour. They had a long way to go. As they traveled, Cruz explained more about the trip. "In old times the tribe would leave the high country. It was colder and more snow then, I think. They would leave about this time or maybe a little later and go down to the river where the winter is warm."

Ben knew this. The elevation where the Colorado River leaves the Grand Canyon is about 1100 feet. The tribe would go farther down the river, nearly to California, and stay at an elevation closer to five hundred feet. Each spring and again each fall they would migrate back and forth, high to low—low to high, living on meat from deer, elk and antelope in the summer and fish, quail, dove and bighorn sheep in the winter. The trek was hard, but life, in general, was good. Sometimes people died on these journeys. These were the grave sites Herman Cruz wanted to check.

Just past noon they rode across Buck and Doe Road, the gravel highway that led north from Peach Springs. It would take a tourist to the Grand Canyon Skywalk where one could walk on the glass-bottomed arc out over the canyon rim. Cruz and Ben rode west.

Northern Arizona is a series of plateaus. Just west of the reservation boundary is the extension of the Mogollon Rim—the Grand Wash Cliffs. It is cut by numerous canyons that lead into the dry lake below: Red Lake.

They stopped at the entrance to one of these canyons. Ben removed his Resistol straw hat and wiped his forehead with his right forearm. A single cotton ball cloud hung in an otherwise clear sky. From his vantage point it appeared as though it was pierced by the jet trail that ran in a perfectly straight line from horizon to horizon.

Herman Cruz waited. When Ben replaced the hat, Cruz said, "See that little cliff at the top of the ridge? The one with the big crack to the right?"

"I see it"

"Remember it. That is where Chief Ta'Yallanah now dwells. He died young. Just before they left the river, he got a nasty cut on his foot. It became infected and this is as far as he got."

Cruz stared at the cliff for a long moment then looked all around. "My grandfather stood right here. He was a boy, then. My father told me my grandfather and two other men waited for a few days. They placed the body in a crack in the rocks and covered it with stones. They watched the vultures and coyotes to make sure they couldn't get to it. Then they walked on.

Ben looked all around and memorized the place. Herman Cruz did not seem inclined to go closer to examine the grave.

They left the reservation and rode on into the canyon. About half way down they found a road that led to a spring. Cruz rode past the rancher's drinker about two hundred yards, pulled up and began to unsaddle. They led the horses to the water and hobbled them in deep grass. While Cruz cooked, Ben refilled the canteens and carried a canvas bag of water to clean up after their meal.

After the utensils had been put away, Ben said, "I guess we can have a drink now. We're a long way from my jurisdiction." He extracted a bottle of Jim Beam from his saddlebag and held it up to Cruz.

"I knew I could count on the U.S Army," he said as he held out a tin cup. "Thank you."

They each had two fingers as they rested against the packs. Ben felt better than he had since his injury. He unrolled his bed and soon fell into a deep sleep.

The next morning, Cruz's stirring around awakened Ben in the darkness, but his training was embedded in his every cell, so he was instantly alert. His hand went to the Glock 17 he kept beside his bedroll. After a moment he realized that it his old friend was preparing breakfast and breaking camp at the same time. This embarrassed Ben. Sleeping in wasn't like him.

The sunlight had not reached into the canyon when they broke camp and rode on. They came to a barbed wire fence. Cruz turned right and rode no more than fifty feet before he dismounted.

"The ranchers know I do this," he said as he opened a well-concealed temporary gate. After they had passed through, Ben helped Herman Cruz wire the fence together. Their tracks were the only obvious signs of their crossing.

They rode on across the dry lake toward the Cerbat Mountains. Twice Cruz had pointed out graves and twice Ben carefully noticed the landmarks and memorized the location. It was not necessary. Cruz didn't know about the GPS receiver. It might have upset the old man if he knew Ben kept a record of their journey, but he feared he would miss one of the graves, and it was possible his old friend wouldn't be around for another trip.

On the third day, they rode high into the Cerbat Mountains.

"Cerbat is the old pai name for bighorn sheep. Now no sheep are left," Cruz explained.

The weather held. The heavens remained clear and the wind calm. Bees were thick in the late-blooming flowers and shrubs.

"When you say pai, do you mean our tribe or all the people?" Ben asked.

"That's a tough question. I mean all the people we were connected to in the beginning. This may be a little vague, but my heart knows what I mean."

They continued in silence. After a few hundred yards, Cruz pulled up and pointed to the south. "That peak is called Mount Tipton by the whites. It is the highest point in these mountains and beyond that is Cherum Peak. That one is named for one of our chiefs. I'm not sure where his grave is."

Cruz dismounted and stretched his legs and back. "Once deer were plentiful on this mountain. Then came the war with the whites. They trapped our warriors up here. They had to kill off most of the game to survive. Times were bad. Finally, the animals were gone and the whites starved us out."

Ben started to ride forward, but Cruz stopped him. "I don't think we should ride across this place." He said nothing more, so Ben just nodded. If his friend had something to add, he would say it. In his own time.

The old man sighed and remounted. "This is as far as we need to go in these mountains. Now we can start back. We will go a different way. I want to show you what to look for in Meriwhitica Canyon."

They dismounted several times during the next day to use the Cruz's secret gates. That night they camped on the east edge of the Joshua tree forest near the north end of Red Lake. The next day they rode up a steep canyon to the top of the Grand Wash Cliffs. Ben knew this area. They were near Garnet Mountain. He knew of a jeep trail which led from a Mohave County road, Antares Road, up another canyon to the top of the plateau and joined up with Buck and Doe Road. Cruz did not take this easy route. He chose the steeper, rougher canyon. This pleased Ben, for a reason he didn't quite understand. Once on top they crossed Buck and Doe Road and camped inside the reservation.

"Now we can kill a deer if we want," Cruz said. "We need more meat."

When Ben didn't comment, the old fellow smiled. "There is a lot of the white man in you now, Benjamin. I think it may be a good thing. I could kill a deer and you would go along with it, but you wouldn't like that idea. We would have to waste a lot of meat." He opened one of his packs. "I have a lot more jerky. I'm just messing with you."

"Well, I have a joke for you," Ben countered. "We ran out of whiskey last night. What is the old warrior planning to do about that?"

"No whiskey allowed on the reservation so no problem. Now I won't break the law and have the police after me. Besides, we have plenty of water."

Before it got dark Herman checked the horse's hooves. The pack horse had a loose shoe which Ben fixed. Otherwise, the animals were in good shape. Herman's way with horses never failed to impress him, and he picked up many pointers along the way. His old friend still continued to mentor him.

"Today we reach our final destination. We will only get within about a half mile but with the field glasses we can get a good look," Cruz said as they saddled to leave. "We will still camp again at least once before we get home."

They rode along the south rim of Meriwhitica Canyon until they reached a promontory at a sharp bend where Meriwhitica joins Spencer Canyon. They hobbled the horses on some good grass and walked to an overlook.

"What happened down there?" Ben asked as they settled down with their binoculars.

Cruz looked down and to the right at the muddy water of the Colorado River. "This is a good time for the tourists—the river-runners. The water is high and covers the rocks and rapids. Their rafts will find smooth going."

They sat in silence once again as Cruz contemplated the question. Ben watched a hawk wheeling around looking for lunch. Another beautiful day on the Coconino Plateau in Northern Arizona. He could feel autumn approaching in the air, the juniper-scented air.

Finally, Cruz got around to answering. "A white rancher lived down there once," he said, pointing to the bright green thicket around Merwhitica Springs. "He leased the entire reservation from the government. Some of our people worked for him and lived down there, too. I think they at some spoiled food. Many died. None of the whites, though. I can show you where they are buried. The council doesn't allow permits for the whites to go down there except for certain special exceptions. It is a sacred place. And besides," he added with a smile. "there are many ghosts down there now."

Cruz suddenly frowned and picked up his binoculars. His old eyes couldn't see anything clearly at this distance, but a flash of light caught his attention. Ben picked up on the reaction and lifted his binoculars.

"Someone is down there," Cruz muttered. "This is not good."

As they studied the canyon floor, they discovered two tents hidden in the shadow of a ledge. A man sat smoking in the shade near the spring. He appeared to be guarding the tents. As they watched, a second man and a woman stepped into view and talked to the guy in the folding chair. Then the woman went into one of the tents. She returned holding the arm of a second female. This one suddenly jerked away, but one of the men caught her. He yanked her around and made threatening gestures. Then the first woman took her behind some bushes where she relieved herself.

"You are right, my friend. Not good." Ben said as the scene played out. He scanned the area along the river and discovered a boat hidden where the canyon intersects the water.

"They have a boat, Herman. It must be a jet. They came up the river with a captive."

"That's what I see," Cruz responded. "We should ride out and get help."

Ben put his glasses down and smiled. "I am the police chief here. This is my jurisdiction, and now you are my patrolman. I say we rescue that girl and get her out of there."

Cruz was skeptical. "You were a Ranger and a hero, but those days are in the past. Now you are a cop with a bum leg. What do you think we could do?"

Ben's smile widened. "By now you have noticed my leg isn't as bad as I let on. I do this to fool people into believing I may not be able to do much in a fight. It's a trick. I have a plan. Want to hear it?"

"I like a good plan. What do you have in mind?"

After removing the packs and picketing the spare horse, they rode together at a fast trot and in about half an hour found where Ben could enter the canyon. He traded his .270 deer rifle for Herman's .30-30. Then he took a canvas bag with a few supplies and a canteen of water and started down the steep slope.

Cruz went a half mile out of his way before returning to the observation post. He took his folding bucket and crawled into a narrow crack in a rock wall. He filled the bucket with cool, fresh water from a tanque. After watering his horses, he went to get the others. Then he returned to the natural cistern and finished the chore. Now there was nothing to do but wait.

Meriwhitica Canyon runs west to east. Ben entered near the west end. By the time he reached the dry wash in the bottom his leg throbbed, but it was the stiffness more than the pain that nagged at him. He briefly wondered at the wisdom of the decision to leave the cane.

Cruz tried to work out a problem. Cell service didn't reach here but the calculator on his phone still functioned. He dug around in his saddle bags and pulled out a USGS Quadrangle Map.

Cruz loved maps. He could sit for hours studying a map and envision any place in great detail. This, however, was not a memory exercise. He scaled the horizontal distance to the spring at almost a half mile. From the contour lines, he estimated the drop in elevation to be about two thousand feet. He also knew that shooting uphill or downhill significantly affected the aiming point. The rifle would always shoot high. His challenge was more complicated than simply holding a bit lower aiming point at a short range target. Cruz had never encountered such a problem.

Is the true length of the shot the horizontal or the slope distance. Cruz had little formal education but was remarkably intelligent. He closed his eyes and tried to envision what would happen when he pulled the trigger. The mental image was unclear. He had never shot at anything much over one hundred-fifty yards.

Gravity. I need to know how far the round will drop. This bullet will leave the rifle at about twenty-seven hundred feet per second and then start slowing down. I guess it will take about two seconds for it to reach the bottom.

Herman used his Leatherman utility tool to remove a bullet from the cartridge case. He held it straight out and let go. "Damn. That was fast. I need more height," he muttered. He climbed on a large rock and repeated the experiment from about ten feet high.

Still fast. By the time that damn bullet gets to the bottom, it will drop forty or fifty feet, I guess. He briefly recalled something about the acceleration of gravity but pushed it from his mind. He realized the futility of this experiment. "To hell with it. I'll just shoot and see where it hits and then adjust," he said to the uninterested horses.

It was nearly dark when Ben arrived at the point he had selected from above. It was better than he expected. The afternoon sun had warmed the rocks and held the temperature up. He made a dry camp in a smooth depression on the northern wall of the canyon. His only protection from the elements was the nylon windbreaker he had tied around his waist. It would be a cold night, and he couldn't risk a fire.

The next morning, Ben had already moved to the shady side before the sunlight hit the canyon bottom. He moved from cover to cover as he approached the tents. Cruz watched this from high above, wishing they had a better way to communicate than just hand signals. The captive moved toward Ben and Cruz could not be sure his companion knew this. The girl seemed to be exploring.

Ben saw the girl. He had watched her for several minutes and decided she must be a teenager. He crept forward and waited behind a boulder. As the girl stepped past, he reached out and pulled her to him, his hand over her mouth.

"Shh. I'm a friend. I'm here to help," he whispered. "Don't make any noise. He turned the wide-eyed girl loose. She spun around and kicked him hard in the shin. Then she screamed.

"Ow! Damn. Hey." Ben yelled, taken completely by surprise.

The girl started running and screaming.

The kidnappers sprinted into view, so Cruz fired. The noise echoed around in the canyon making it impossible for them to know where the shot originated. Cruz didn't see where the bullet hit, so he fired again. People screamed and ran in all directions. Ben watched in confusion. So did Cruz. It resembled a scene from The Keystone Kops.

Ben watched as the girl tripped and measured her length in the dry wash. She came up spitting sand. One of the kidnappers tried to hide in the brush at the spring just as Cruz fired again. One of the young men ran from the brush straight at Ben as though he didn't see him.

But he did. "Hold your fire. Stop the shooting. We have no guns," he yelled as he waved his arms around like one of those goofy air-filled men seen in used car lots.

Ben stepped into full view and held up his rifle. He waved to Cruz indicating for him to cease fire. Then he walked out past the terrified young man and over to the girl now sitting in the wash and picking sand from her skinned elbows.

"Who the hell are you," the girl demanded?

"I'm the law here," Ben answered. Technically this wasn't true. They were inside the boundary of the Grand Canyon National Park but he figured it was close enough.

"Then get your ass out of here go catch some criminals," she said as she spit out more sand.

Ben smiled. "Okay. Just as soon as I see your permit to enter a sacred site, Miss...I didn't catch the name."

"My father's lawyers will crush your nuts, Mr. Cop."

Ben left the girl picking out grains of sand and went to a young woman who was badly skinned up from trying to go through the dense brush at the spring. She sat on a rock with tears running down her face. Ben showed her his badge.

"Name?" he asked.

"Julie Winslow. I'm a friend of Carrie's."

"Carrie is the little witch with dirt in her mouth?"

Julie nodded.

"Just what the hell are you people doing here?"

Julie started to answer when one of the young men interrupted. "Don't say a word, Julie."

"It's over, Don. I don't know why she thought this would work."

Don kicked a rock, winched at the pain in his foot, and went toward a tent.

"Stay where I can see you, Don," Ben told him. "You don't want the shooting to start again."

Don found a rock and sat.

"What's the deal, Julie."

She sucked in a shuddering breath and told him. "Carrie's dad owns a casino in Vegas. He didn't like the way she behaved and became so he came down on her. She thought if she were kidnapped she could cash in and get her father's sympathy at the same time. She talked us into helping out. We used my uncle's boat to come up the river."

Ben chuckled. "Hell of a plan. I have another question. Yesterday I saw one of the boys yanking Carrie around. I felt sure she was a prisoner. What was that all about?"

"Oh, that. Carrie got upset about the sanitation situation. She bitched about having no chemical toilet. Walt just set her straight, that's all."

Ben chuckled. "A real pioneer woman. Now you guys get on your best walking shoes and all the water you can carry. You're in for a long, hard day."

When Herman Cruz saw the little caravan start up the canyon, he loaded the gear and went to meet them at the head of the canyon. Three hours later the exhausted group topped out and met the grinning old Hualapai.

"Okay, Ben. I think this is a good time for you to get the satellite phone and GPS receiver out of you pack and call for a ride. These city kids aren't good for much more walking."

Ben shook his head in disbelief and complied. His old friend didn't miss anything.

"That was some Ranger attack I watched. You are a true warrior," Cruz grinned.

"That was some good shooting, too, Old Man. You barely hit the ground." They both laughed and hunted some shade.

"You assholes just wait. My father will deal with this. We are not treated this way unless somebody pays. Get ready for a massive lawsuit." Carrie was still belligerent after the hard climb.

Herman and Ben ignored her. An hour later two police SUVs arrived. The tired, dirty and sweat-stained intruders were taken into official custody.

A week passed since the kids were turned over to the Las Vegas police for staging a fake kidnapping. The ransom note had disturbed Carrie's father just as she had planned. He had to discharge the small army he had hired to find his daughter.

Ben drove his patrol car out to Herman's place. He found the old man rubbing down the pack horse after a workout.

"Come in, Benjamin. I'll fix us some coffee." They went into Cruz' little house. "What brings you all the way out here? Going to arrest me for drinking whiskey on the reservation?"

"That's a thought, but no. I got a call from Burton Vistachi—Miss Carrie's dad. He thanked me for finding her and offered a reward. I told him anything he wanted to donate to benefit the tribe would be welcome. He said he would consider that."

Ben poured coffee. "He also told me that Carrie had become a problem. She started running with a tough crowd, and he feared they used drugs."

Herman joined Ben at the table. "What will he do."

"He took her credit cards. He may put her in the public school system. There are several things he is considering. Like putting her to work. She needs to earn her way." Ben took another sip of the potent brew. "I told him he might seek professional help. Or find something to keep her occupied. Something she enjoys."

"Good advice. By the way. When you gave me your rifle and took mine, why didn't you tell me how to aim down that canyon? I still lose sleep trying to figure it out."

"I was Special Forces—a Green Beret. We have special sniper rifles. We use a spotter with all kinds of gadgets. When we're ready to shoot, all we have to do is put the crosshair on the target and hold steady. I had no idea what to tell you. I just wanted to carry yours because it's lighter."

"Good thing the ghosts were on your side."

More About Roy—

Roy Voss retired from a career of designing and building high-pressure pipelines. The work took him to five continents and once, in a thirty-day period, resulted in two trips around the world—one going east and the other west. What was once an obsession with golf has morphed into a love of writing. In addition to the self-published novel, PAYBACK, Roy has completed six other unpublished novels based on incidents from those travels. He now lives with his wife, Bobbi, in a country home just outside of Palestine, Texas.

THE OBIT
By Roy Voss

I was surprised, a little shocked, and saddened to find her obituary, but there it was:

STUPID B. EVERBODILY

Question: What can a can can?
The kitchen of Ms.
Everbodily always smelled
of pewter and spice and if
she had been able to cook,
would probably have
smelled better...

I wiped my cheeks remembering the beautiful person that had been Lisa Harmon, the vibrant young lady who became known as Stupid. She died at age twenty-seven from a heart condition which had been predicted to kill her as a kid, but somehow she just laughed her way through it.

I asked her one day, while we sat at her kitchen table enjoying coffee and cake, "Lisa, what possessed you to change your name to Stupid? That's what's stupid!"

She just laughed as she so often did and said, "You know, I just started thinking one night while looking up at the moon— men have been there! There are few citizens smart enough to build a vehicle to transport men to our moon. They fly there, unload ground transportation, drive around and bag up a bunch of moon rocks, then get back into their spacecraft and fly home." She fiddled with her long, auburn locks and continued with a beguiling smile. "I'm not even sure which way the moon goes around the earth. It got me thinking. I was in the top ten percent of my class in high school and graduated cum laude from college. But basically, I'm pretty stupid compared to smart people, so is most everyone else. I decided to identify myself with my own kind."

"But, Lisa..."

"Don't call me Lisa—please. I know my place."

"Okay, but I refuse to call you Stupid. You are one of the sharpest people I've ever met."

Her smile widened. "You don't know many people, do you?"

I snorted in exasperation.

"No, really! Think about it," she said. "People are killing each other off all over the world in the name of religion. What can be dumber than that? Some dingbat doesn't like the way I worship so he thinks he needs to kill me. It's bad enough that he wants to make me wear a burka, no?"

I nodded in agreement but didn't interrupt.

"Then there's partisan politics. Politicians are screwing over people just so their political party can one-up the other. I bet they keep score. And if that's not bad enough, what about political correctness?

To me, that's what really takes the prize. Sheesh!" She took a bite of cake. "Umm, this is good!"

"But that's no reason for you to call yourself stupid, my dear. I think it's brilliant of you just to recognize all the things that you think are wrong."

"Wrong? Don't get me started. How about all the terrorist organizations? I see people with a fifteenth-century mindset carrying twenty-first-century weapons. And I can't possibly comprehend how a person could begrudge a girl an education just because she's female. Insane! Even worse, what about mothers who drown their babies? What about all the domestic abuse?"

As she went on I sipped coffee and ate some of the cake, then interjected, "But Li...my dear, this isn't you. You are not the stupid one. I think the correct word for most of this is ignorance rather than stupidity. I'm not sure if these bozos truly believe the crap they spew or just do it because they can. For instance, check this out...I read an article the other day instructing how a Muslim can beat his wife without leaving marks. Another piece told about their divorces. These guys divorce their wives for anything. One woman put too much salt in her husband's food, so he divorced her. Another was slow in bringing water when he asked so out she goes. The list went on." I took another bite. "Don't forget insanity. Mothers who kill their babies are completely nuts. You know that."

I remembered how she stood and went to the window, hands behind her back, her fingers interlaced, just staring outside at the world. She sighed. "Think about our bodies. Think about what magnificent organisms we are. Trees are pretty complex, but compared to us, they're just a stack of cellulose. Think about your eyes, your ears and while you're at it, and most importantly, your brain. How did such a beautiful organism come to be? We are given our senses and our ability to think and reason, to move about, to do and build. So what do we do? We turn to greed. Whatever happened to the Golden Rule? Do you know it appears in one way or another in almost every religion? If that one simple rule were the universal code, then all would be well, and I could be Lisa again. But no...it just can't happen because we are all too stupid. Humanity can never live in harmony, can it? Never! That's because people will always want what someone else has and would rather take it than work for it."

"Are you thinking socialism?" I asked.

She turned back from the window and nearly melted me with her smile. "No, of course not, that could never work. Socialism removes all initiative. What I'm talking about is being satisfied with what you can do for yourself. If someone has more than you because they work for it, they deserve it, and if you could do the same but don't, then you should do without. You just have to accept the fact that you just don't deserve something for nothing. If you're too lazy to or unambitious, you have to live with it. That's your choice, and it's really not asking too much."

"No exceptions?" I asked.

"Oh, yes. There will always be some exceptions, I suppose. People who have handicaps might need some assistance, that sort of thing. I don't claim to have a master plan all worked out. I couldn't. That's how I know I'm one of the stupid."

"You make it sound like the earth is a terrible place to live." I finished my cake. "By the way, this coffee is exceptional."

"It's the only place we have, but I know I will leave it soon, and I can hope, at least, there is a better place."

"I wish you wouldn't talk that way."

Again the smile. "Does it make you uncomfortable to talk about death? Your day will come, too, you know."

"Not really uncomfortable, but it isn't my favorite subject."

"I have been blessed. I've lived a very full and happy life and experienced things that most people on earth never will. I've flown in a fighter jet and ridden on a submarine. Best of all, I will not die a virgin."

I blushed but didn't comment. She wasn't talking about me and I sure didn't intend to pry.

She joined me at the table. "If we were to sit here and make a list of all the stupid things people do we would never leave this table. They're happening faster than we can write them down." She tasted another bite of cake. It was store-bought but better than if she had tried to prepare it. "Since 9-11 life has changed, too. I can see where profiling might work, at least in some cases. Would you mind being profiled?"

"I've never given it much thought."

"I got profiled at the airport recently. I was flying to Houston and wore a floor-length dress. I got pulled out of line and patted down to make sure I didn't have a bomb hidden under it. I didn't mind."

I had to laugh along and added, "My daughter and her family were flying out of Toledo early one morning. My granddaughter had turned four that day. Security pulled her out of line, frisked her, and x-rayed her teddy bear. Poor little Mia—spread-eagled against a wall and barely able stay awake. I guess that is the opposite of profiling, but it is nonetheless, ridiculous."

She nodded in concurrence. "I suppose the logic there is she could have been carrying the bomb for her parents."

I scoffed. "Like what parents are gonna blow up an airplane with their kids aboard?"

"You're bolstering my thesis. Maybe you should change your name, too. And about the coffee, you know I can't boil water, but since I discovered the Keurig system all I have to do is pour filtered water and push a button. I can do that."

I was laughing when I woke up. The dream was in color, and I could easily recall every detail as if it was real. My wife was already at the breakfast table reading the newspaper and drinking her own coffee. She looked up and smiled as I joined her.

"I just had the weirdest dream," I said. "And it was hilarious." We laughed hard when I told her the name of the deceased and the goofy question in the obituary. I related the story in great detail and wondered what it all meant.

My wife gave me a condescending smile. "Well, dreams are strange things as best," she said. "I don't believe anyone knows exactly what they're all about. I remember my eighth-grade teacher explaining them as memory strings that dangle down from our brains and get twisted together. She told us that while we sleep the strings are pulled up to show us the scene like a movie. Her idea is that they try to make sense but usually come out all screwed up because of the tangles. I guess that makes as much sense as anything I've heard."

I poured my coffee which seemed somehow inferior to Stupid's and began to peruse the news, but a creepy feeling kept interrupting.

"Honey, what if she was right?"

My wife looked up from the paper with a quizzical expression. "What do you mean?"

"Think about it. That one simple rule would mean peace and harmony to the entire world except for the true loonies and there's nothing can be done about them. Even wild animals have a certain amount of crazies."

Her brow furrowed as she stared at me. "Drink your coffee. Read the paper. It was a dream. We had a good laugh, now forget it. A perfect world wouldn't be perfect, they say."

But I couldn't leave it. Why hadn't this ever occurred to me in the proper context before? Sure, we were all taught the Golden Rule as kids, but it just seemed like something else to remember rather than something to actually put into practice— something that might be on an exam.

"Do you think it was some kind of a message?" I asked.

She heaved a sigh. "It was just a dream. Your nephew is a psychologist. Call him. I'm trying to work this crossword puzzle. That's enough on my plate this morning."

I attempted to read the news again, but the haunting continued. "I may decide to change my name."

"To Stupid?"

"Maybe. Something like that."

She tapped the pen (she works crossword puzzles in ink) and thought about it. "Okay, I see what you're saying. Mankind is flawed. There're smart people and dumb people, and I don't know the ratio, but I imagine the loonies are way more numerous than we realize. Just look how many people text and drive. Try not to be so worked up. It's not good for your blood pressure." She went back to the puzzle, then added, "If you want to worry about something, concentrate on our septic tank problem. Installing an aerobic system isn't gonna be cheap."

In a flash, my mind shifted gears. She always has a way of putting things into perspective. I took a drink of coffee which tasted very good all of a sudden, but then I began to cloud over again.

She noticed. "Okay, look at it this way. We're doing the very best we can to survive. We try hard to be good neighbors and good people. You are not stupid. Your brother may be, but you're not."

I grinned. My brother is terrific, and she knows it.

She went on, "You want to know the real message in the dream? I'll tell you. You missed the point completely. She told you flat out, and you barely touched on it."

"Yeah? What was that?"

"She said best of all; she wouldn't die a virgin. Neither will you. Now shut up and drink your coffee."

She's really smart, my wife.

THE UNEXPECTED

A True Account
By Mark Enlow

I thought it would be another typical day. I was working at the bank as the branch's unofficial head teller—all of the duties, none of the pay. There would be, as usual, customers who were red-faced, and some who were irate, because their accounts were overdrawn. Lunch would come and go. Some tellers would not be able to balance their ponderous mounds of paperwork at the end of the day. We would later, close in the afternoon, and go home, however it was not going to be "business as usual" on this day.

Everything was going smoothly including the drive-in window operation Tom and I were working. Three lobby teller positions were open as well. Customers were waited on in a courteous and prompt manner.

The interaction between the tellers and the customers in the lobby was made somewhat difficult because of the one-inch thick bulletproof glass. It surrounded the entire office and teller line. On this particular day there were three female tellers waiting on customers in the lobby.

When the rare moment occurred that the lobby was empty of customers, the usual jokes and kidding amongst each other would arise.

April would say to Tom, "I'll bet you five-thousand dollars, that the Redskins will beat Houston on Sunday." She would hold up five-thousand dollars and wave it at Tom.

Tom would reply, "I'll bet you five-thousand and raise you five-thousand that they won't." He would confidently place the money on the counter as he played along.

We were in our own "little world" here in this glass capsule, filled with what we sometimes thought of as "Monopoly" money.

Meanwhile in the lobby, a customer left the manager's office looking bewildered. He was studying his checkbook as he slammed the heavy glass door behind him.

Sally commented, "I guess Bob wouldn't approve cashing his check since the account is already overdrawn."

Another customer approached the office's smooth-edged porthole cut in the thick, clear glass. Bob arose and let a man in a long, brown, trench coat in. The customer strode toward the restrooms and disappeared inside.

Just after, my attention was turned towards another teller having trouble totaling a car dealer's rather large deposit of musty smelling bills and checks spread on the counter.

I glanced up to see Bob, who now had a startled expression across his face. The customer with the rumpled, brown trench coat, who had gone into the restroom moments earlier, now held a dull, black, six-shot revolver to Bob's head.

The robber waved the heavy gun nervously at

us. The gun with the nickel-sized hole at the end of it shook as the robber's hand trembled. His finger twitched on the trigger. Pointing to an empty white, canvas coin bag he demanded, "Put all the money in the bag, now!"

Bob complied and tried to give him ones, fives, and the special marked money. April, standing in the middle of my frozen co-workers, tripped the silent alarm with the foot button. The gray security cameras started clicking faster in the now vast silence.

I took a step to one side to close a money drawer. A sliver of fear penetrated my stomach as the hold-up man waved the gun in my direction. "Don't move!" he bellowed.

"Hand me the bag!" the robber demanded of Bob. "Now, stay where you are!" The gunman backed his way down the teller line towards the office door, waving the revolver at eye level toward us. When he reached the lobby he ran to the outside exit door.

Bob and I followed to see if we could get a vehicle description and a tag number, but we were both surprised to see the bank robber had plotted his escape. He walked out of the parking lot double-time, crossing a four-lane highway intersection nearby. Bob turned and told me, "Go back to the bank, lock the front door, and wait for the police."

Bob continued to trail the gunman on foot, at a distance, into a residential neighborhood. That was where the hold-up man had stashed his getaway car to avoid any description of it. Bob observed the make and model of the car and noted the tag number. We found out later from authorities that the effort to obtain a vehicle description had led nowhere. The car had been stolen and it was found abandoned a few miles away.

The bank robbery was over. The hold-up seemed like an eternity, but only lasted sixty-seconds. The bank filled with an army of uniformed police, FBI agents, and bank officials. The nervous bank robber was long gone. He had escaped with what the newspapers would later say, was a considerable amount of money. However, more importantly everyone at the bank branch had survived, unharmed. I often wondered if the robber had ever been captured.

My answer was forthcoming. Years later an FBI agent came to show me some pictures of the gunman. Unfortunately, it had been years. I could not positively identify him as the unexpected cause that interrupted a typical day.

More About Mark—
Mark Enlow grew up in Maryland, just outside Washington D.C. He worked in the beautiful capital city of Washington for most of his career. Always ready for new experiences, he received his private pilot license, real estate license, and worked his way up to an engineering assistant in telecommunications. All along life's way though, especially after college literature accolades by a professor, he had a desire to write stories, never finding the time until now. He say's "The best part about writing is, creating experiences on paper that both entertains the reader and transports them to a

different place for a little while." He has completed his first novel, an 85,000 word science fiction adventure novel and is currently seeking a literary agent for representation leading to its publication. He lives in Arizona with his wife, Janet, and his canine/administrative assistant, Casey. Mark can be reached at: MarkE.Author@outlook.com

A LESSON IN TIME
A True Account
By Anne Marie Kensington

After moving to a new school, I noticed my sweet children Jimmy—in the fourth grade, and Jackie in seventh—most days came through our apartment door with sad faces. Both of them experiencing the typical trials that come with being new kids in school, but Jimmy's issues troubled me most.

In this larger school, a new kid was easy prey for the class bully, especially if the new kid had the last name of Sanchez. In Jimmy's young innocent life he had not yet encountered bigotry with his Norwegian-Swedish-Italian-Mexican heritage.

One day after school, he said, "Mom, can we talk?" nervously twirling a pen on the table.

"Of course, sweetheart." I sat down by him.

"Does the word 'spic' mean some kind of a bad Mexican person?" he continued.

"Why? Who said that?" I questioned, while trying not to over-react.

"Every day Davey Cramer and his friends call me that and they also call me 'wetback' and 'beaner'. Why do they call me those names, Mom?"

With a troubled heart I took a deep breath and said a quick prayer. "I'm going to need some help with this one, Lord."

The day this bully and his pack stuffed him into his locker, was the day it became a problem needing a mother's meddling. They even shut the door with him inside. Jimmy said, "My buddy Jeff stayed behind and helped me get out."

"Did you tell your teacher?" I asked.

"No," he replied, "I didn't want more trouble." And so it happened again and again.

Jimmy was short for a nine year old. The leader of the bullying pack, Davey was taller than everyone, almost a foot taller than Jimmy, and nearly a year older.

The time had come for me to talk to his teacher, Mrs. Johnson. But when I explained his problem, she just said, "I haven't seen any behavior like you are describing."

"Well, Jimmy said it has happened several times. I know he isn't making it up. Could you please try to catch them in the act and make them stop?" Trying not to sound demanding.

She told me, quite matter-of-factly, "Young David comes from a prestigious family. Being new in town, you may not realize he is the son of the city attorney."

"I did know," I answered, "but certainly his parents won't condone such behavior. I'm sure they'll want to discipline him."

Mrs. Johnson stated, "I will certainly discourage that behavior if I ever do catch them."

"Yes, you be sure to discourage them," was my mocking response as I turned to walk away. I could tell from her tone we would need to solve this one ourselves.

A few blocks away at the Junior High, Jackie was hoping to win friends in her new school, but both the boys and girls of good quality in her grade were reluctant to welcome this unproven new girl into their groups. The groups who welcomed her eagerly were not the kind of friends she ever brought home. This group lied to their mothers and hung out at the mall.

"I guess I'll have to become a super athlete at school before Grant will ever talk to me," she whined one night at dinner.

"Who's Grant," I asked with a smile? I was so happy she was sharing.

"Just the cutest boy in the whole school," she answered. "He's out for football and he sits right across from me in English. He's very popular, but he doesn't even know I'm alive."

"Hmmm. You both need some happy experiences. Let me think. Do you guys remember a couple of years ago when I went to see Zig Ziglar speak in Minneapolis? You both told me when I came home, that I was a walking Ziglar quote machine."

One thing Ziglar taught was that when there is more bad than good, ignore the bad and concentrate only on the good. Then turn your focus and your energy to those good things. That idea was from his book, *See You at the Top*.

I presented my idea. "I'm giving you guys an assignment. We'll discuss the results at dinner tomorrow. For one entire school day, look only for good things. If bad things happen, tell yourself, 'that's not what I'm looking for. My search is for something good.' Don't even acknowledge the bad. That's not going to be included in our dinner conversation. I'll do the same thing. I'll set the table as though we're expecting company. We'll be the important guests, telling the stories about the day's good events."

I realized this was risky plan. What if nothing good happened? I hoped and prayed for the best.

The next day they both walked through the door with enormous smiles and faces ripe with anticipation.

We ate early. None of us could wait to share our stories.

After saying grace and dishing up our food, I asked, "Who wants to begin?"

Jimmy proudly volunteered. "Today my music teacher picked me to sing a solo for the Christmas Concert." What a great compliment for him, and a terrific confidence builder.

"But guess who sang the solo last year," he quizzed excitedly. Then without waiting, he blurted out, "Davey!" and a proud smile covered his face.

"Davey Cramer," I asked?

"Yes, and he looked bummed when he didn't get chosen again this year," he answered.

We clinked our glasses of ginger ale together and reveled in his good news.

Jackie was next. "Grant Colson, the cute boy in English, helped me pick up the pile of books I dropped coming down the stairs." Her smile stretched from earlobe to earlobe.

"And that's not all. He asked if I'm going to the school dance on Friday night. Can I go, mom?"

My best hopes were exceeded. Jackie had dismissed her embarrassment at dropping books on the stairs. She focused on and shared only that the cutest boy in English, not only noticed her, but also made an obvious effort to help her.

Our glasses clinked again. I saw hope and excitement in their eyes.

"Yes, you can go to the dance on Friday. I'll drive you and pick you up," I agreed happily.

They really got it! Both of them! We all followed up our great days with our fun celebration. It felt so good. Seeing smiles on their faces was heartwarming.

Ziglar is a genius, I was thinking! The first dinner in weeks that wasn't clouded with hopelessness.

"What's your story, Mom?" Jackie asked.

"Well, when I went to the mailbox today, there was a large order and a check for Cambridge from a new customer who says she'll order regularly." At that time I sold the Cambridge diet drink. This was perfect timing! There were happy faces all around.

Jimmy adored Kevin, my current boyfriend. Kevin, a city cop, who played the guitar, had been patiently teaching Jimmy a few chords.

"Bullying rarely turns out well," Kevin said after hearing Jimmy's sad tale. "But, do you know that it's Davey's dad who sometimes has to defend my arrests in court? It will have to be a well-kept family secret that this advice came from me." Then Kevin offered his plan.

"You're going to have to fight this kid," He began.

"Oh no! Jimmy is not a fighter!" I squealed. "That will never work."

Kevin continued, "You will have to land the first punch and hit him hard. I'm sorry, but you're going to have to hurt him. Plus, it'll be best if you can hit him in the nose so there will be blood."

Jimmy's eyes seemed to be locked wide open. I could see his mind picturing it all.

In the coming days, we had several conversations about the proposed fight. I needed to be sure Jimmy really believed he would win.

He had to win!

Jimmy punched the air as he walked through our apartment. His grunts and facial expressions declared his serious preparation for the big day. After some role-playing with Kevin, Jimmy was ready.

Of course I worried, but the bullying had to stop and we had tried everything else. If this didn't go well, it would be even more traumatic for Jimmy. But, if successful, he could hold his head high during fifth grade and maybe for the rest of his life.

The challenge went out and the boys set the date. They would meet just off the school property after the final bell at 3:31, the last day of school.

I parked a block away to be close but not too close. My heart convulsed. Jimmy had to win. *Dear Jesus, please be with him. Please help him.*

All of the fourth and fifth graders who didn't have to go home on the school bus, gathered around the corner lot.

Jackie stood ringside; so to speak, ready to cheer her brother on. All year I noticed she was hurting for him, while he endured the bullying. She whooped and hollered for her little brother in the fight of his life.

Wham! The first punch landed on Davey's nose as he leaned in with a cocky taunt. Immediately, blood spurted everywhere. At the sight of his own blood, Davey howled. Jimmy threw another punch. It put Davey on the ground. Jimmy pummeled him until Davey screamed, "Stop! You win!" in a voice loud enough for everyone to hear.

At this declaration, the punching stopped. Jimmy helped him up and began to catch his own breath. His look was that of a proud young victor as he watched Davey limp home sobbing and wiping away blood.

By 3:35 the fight was over. Almost thirty middle-school kids had watched wide-eyed. Many mouthed, "Wow!"

The following years of middle school found the two boys sharing the same classroom but now there was no tension. Davey lost the fear and also the respect of his followers and never again bullied new kids.

Jimmy enjoyed his new reputation of *dragon slayer* and also was delighted to discover that during the school year, he had grown. He was now two inches taller.

Today, Jimmy, a wealthy middle-aged businessman, says he has used Kevin's advice many times in his successful adult life, although more figuratively than literally. He also makes an effort at least one day a month to focus only on the good things that happen.

When the time is right, he says he will pass this wisdom on to his own young boys.

Anne Marie Kensington

GOOD WITCH VS BAD WITCH
A True Account
By Alice Klies

Lately, I've felt toxic, negative thoughts nibble at the walls of my brain. Almost always when this happens, I'm then turned into the 'Wicked Witch of the West.' Now, I don't much enjoy a ride on a tilted broom that sways from side to side, so before I start to stir a cauldron of bubbling misery, I decide to try and correct my own behavior.

Right away, the logical part of my brain assures me that I'm not the Lone Ranger on the subject of negativity. I tell myself that no one is immune to toxic mood swings, and already I make myself feel better!

Just minutes will pass, however, before I, the 'good witch' takes a nosedive off the broom that I adorned with hearts, flowers, and streams of colorful ribbons that flow, to represent goodness. Once again, toxic thoughts start to swirl through my mind.

I struggle financially; I can't go on vacation, Poor me! All my friends are surfing in an ocean, frolicking on a sandy beach or nestling up to a cozy fireplace beneath tall forest trees. Woe is me! I cup my face in my hands. I'm so frustrated. Is this feeling called envy? I want to smack the side of my head with my hand. Since when did life become a competition? My stomach flutters and I know that God just shook His head. He convinces me "Count your own blessings... not someone else's." My rationale perks me up once again. I smile.

I begin to feel down right cheerful until... my daughter sends me a text message. My phone beeps one of those annoying tunes that only a teenager finds fun and refreshing. She tells me that she won't be home for dinner because she is going to visit *him.*

Oh no, the judgmental witch jumps off her broom and bounces up and down on my shoulder. I know that she is toxic. I don't want her to take control of my mind so I start to argue with her.

"He's not really such a bad person. He has probably come from a dysfunctional home and it spills over into *his* negative behavior. I don't know what drives him to be who he is. Besides, judgment is ugly." I intentionally rub at my shoulder, kneading it, to flick the wicked witch to the floor. I shake my head. "Nope, I'm not going there."

For the moment, I've squelched a toxic behavior that comes up frequently in my life. It's one that sneaks up and wiggles itself past my toxic thought barriers. I start to feel better again. The corners of my mouth twitch and force my lips upward. I puff up my chest and square my shoulders.

I settle myself on our cushy couch in the family room. My husband just finished mopping all the floors. Yes, I know. I'm one lucky lady! But as my eyes scan the floors, I'm ashamed, that instead of an urge to embrace my blessing, that I want to get up from the couch and redo hubby's job!

I see specks of dog hair and a small coffee drip that he has missed. Is perfectionism a toxic behavior? Yep! What's wrong with me? "Hey girl... get off the negative witch broom!"

I talk to myself again. I need to remember that what is here today is not going to be the same tomorrow. My perfectionism is a control issue—also negative. I know that flexibility softens my heart and allows playfulness in my words and thoughts. I'm ashamed.

I draw a deep breath, square my shoulders again and turn my gaze away from the coffee spot and dog hair. I stand, embrace my husband, and plant a kiss on his cheek and say, "Thanks' honey." I, the good witch, put the negative bad witch and her broom in a closet and lock the door.

I turn to walk down the hallway to check on laundry that I hear thumping in the dryer. I am more or less confident that I have laid all my toxic feelings of the day to rest. Suddenly I am headed head over heels toward the tile floor. I've tripped over my Golden Retriever and shout as I'm about to know what it feels like at seventy-two to feel my knees make hard contact with a tile floor. I do a face plant and scream, "Why me?"

Is a sense of victimization a type of toxic behavior? Guess I have a lot to work on to conquer toxic behavior. I am a willing student and I do believe an old dog can be taught new tricks. So, for today, I intend to leave the bad witch and her broom in the locked closet and throw away the key.

I will do my best at flying the straight and narrow path on my flower and ribbon laden good witch broom. With God's grace and constant conviction, I intend to conquer the world with love.

KEEP ON KEEPING ON!
A True Account
By Marchelle Perry

There are many different challenges in life. Some are the consequences of choices we make; some are the result of others' actions. Addiction to drugs, sex, alcohol and such, can be overcome with life-long recovery programs. Mental illness, physical illness or injuries can be treated and, hopefully, cured. Marriages can be strengthened or destroyed by any one of these or other circumstances.

One of the most damaging things to a marriage comes from the death of a child. The incidence of divorce after the death of a child is 90% the first year—regardless of the age of the child or cause of death. Families are torn apart by the death and again by the separation of the parents. There is always the chance of suicide by one of the parents or siblings. Surviving children can turn to reckless or unhealthy behaviors because they feel responsible, in some way; that their parents no longer have time for them or that Mom and Dad loved the dead child more. This is the story of my family beating the odds.

June 25, 1983, is our day of infamy. My husband Rad was a truck driver; I was a media assistant in the public schools and I was off for the summer. Our four sons—Ally, 18, who was home from his first year at college; Bucko, 16; Randy, 14 and Ryan, 11 were all looking forward to some good old fashioned summer fun. Ally had gone to a party with his high school friends to catch up on their year. Bucko was packed and ready for a week in the mountains with a friend and his family. His biggest worry was that we would forget to pick him up when we went for our family vacation at our trailer near White Mountain Lake. The evening of the 25th we decided to go to a drive-in movie, not knowing this would be our last night as a whole family.

We never made it to the movies however, because a drunk driver hit our vehicle when we were about 3 miles from home! Without going into all of the gory details, I made the call no parent ever wants to make, or receive. I called Ally and told him to come as quickly as possible—his brother Bucko was dying. Ally came and we were all together one last time and I held my son when he took his last breath. The odd thing was, the Easter song "Jesus Christ is Risen Today" was running through my head.

Bucko was now gone, taken from us at the tender age of sixteen, by a thoughtless, careless, drunk driver! We were left with the deep and terrible pain of grief and sadness—and a son and brother to bury and say our final goodbye's to.

Now we had to get into survival mode.

Thank God for faith, family and friends; all three were and are needed for any hope of keeping it together, individually or as a family. The first year is a jumble of funeral plans, healing from our physical injuries, dealing with insurance companies and the court system, (notice I didn't call it a justice system, for we received none). Pastor Midthun came to the emergency room. His words were comforting, "Jesus is crying with us tonight." The family gathered from wherever they had been and friends were always available with food, hugs and Kleenex. Our brother-in-law, Bill Shafer, gave us wise advice. He told us not to start questioning everything with, "would've, could've, should've." Our parents and sisters never left our sides. We moved together like a cartoon group that was joined at the hip while planning the funeral. Rad and I had input, but made very few decisions. To be honest, we were not capable.

Bucko was killed on a Saturday night. The funeral was on a Wednesday and by Sunday we were holding our nephew/godson, Jeremiah Meyer, at the altar for his baptism. This is when our motto became: *Keep on Keeping on!* Everyone wanted to know how we could manage. All we knew was that we had to provide as normal a life as possible for our surviving sons.

Everyone handles grief and loss in their own way—there is no right way, no wrong way or time limit. I went to grief counseling which was very helpful, not only for my own sanity but to help understand Rad and the boys. People think that once the funeral and courtroom trial are over, life goes back to normal. Wrong—there is never "normal" again. We developed a new normal. I set the table for 5 instead of 6. Ally got his own room instead of having to share. Randy buried his best buddy. Ryan tried to become his brother for a bit—

till he found himself. Rad was on the road, trying not to dwell on the night his son died. Life goes on...

We encouraged Ally to go back to Northern Arizona University. Since hind-sight is perfect, we know now we should have kept him home. He felt guilty for not being with us when we were hit. He kept saying, "...if I had been there..."

I finally told him, "My parent magic couldn't save Bucko, what makes you think your brother magic would have worked?" These are some of the things that no one prepares for.

In the months that followed Ryan, the youngest, told me, "You know, Mom, I've thought about killing myself so I could be with Bucko, but I thought I might not end up in the same place."

We had a discussion about suicide and I told him it had been angels of the Lord who had come to escort Bucko to heaven when he died an innocent victim to someone else's reckless behavior but had Ryan willfully committed suicide, his soul would have been escorted to a dark and dreary place. "Tis far better to live with grief and serve the Lord and have hope that we will all be together again in heaven one day than to confine our souls to the devil's will by committing suicide."

With Ally away at college, Bucko gone, Dad on the road and mom a bit of a basket case, Randy set himself up to be THE MAN of the home. He thought it was his job to protect us all. How did we survive these dynamics? With the grace of God and a lot of hard choices.

Honesty is the best policy whether it's between husband and wife or parents and children.

This is the time to close ranks and realize that we must depend on each other to survive. I got good at telling the family that I was having a bad day and they treated me with kindness. I encouraged others to speak up. Problems cannot be handled if they are hidden. We told the boys that we were over-protective before Bucko was killed and we would be worse now. It made it easier for them to understand when we said, "no." They knew it had nothing to do with trusting them.

Four months after our tragedy, Randy was confirmed in our church. It was extremely difficult, but we had the usual family celebration for him. He deserved it. Again, the question was asked, "How can you do this?" My answer, "How can we not?" This is part of *Keep on Keeping on* —making sure family traditions are carried out.

As time goes on, we continue to celebrate birthdays, graduations, weddings, grandchildren and now great-grandchildren! Rad and I renewed our wedding vows on our 25th Anniversary. For our 50th Anniversary, the boys and their families gave us a wonderful family vacation in Colorado. The most difficult times are Christmas and other major holidays—to this day, I automatically pick up four of whatever for stockings, baskets, etc.

What is the magic we discovered? There is none. No one blames anyone except the drunk for killing Bucko. Just like our country proclaims, we knew we had to stick together or we would all fall apart. Little things don't loom as large anymore. We have suffered the ultimate loss—nothing can hurt like that again. There is no overcoming or recovering after the death of a child, there is only survival and hanging in there together. We continue trusting in God. Our family cares for each other, protects each other and learned to *Keep on Keeping on!*

Rad and I are back to just the two of us again. Ally, Randy and Ryan are good husbands and fathers, two of them are even grandfathers. They have their homes, families and careers. We are very proud of all of them. The sadness creeps in when I think about the "could have been" for Bucko. Would he have fulfilled his desire to be a member of the Cowboy Artists Association? Would he have gotten a job on a ranch or have his own farm or ranch? What kind of husband and father would he have been? It's always there, that little touch of sadness and wistfulness when we talk about our family. But life goes on and so do the challenges. As I write this, Rad has had surgeries and now, radiation treatments for salivary gland cancer but we will *Keep on Keeping on!*

More About Marcy—

I was born July 23, 1942 in New London, Wisconsin. I am the middle of 5 children. I grew up in Oshkosh, Wisconsin, in, what I call, a Norman Rockwell childhood. I graduated from Graveraet High School in Marquette, Michigan, in 1960. Yes, I'm a YUPPER! We moved to Arizona right after graduation. I attended Arizona State University. I met an Arizona native, Rad Perry. We married in 1962 and had 4 sons. I retired from East Valley Institute of Technology (EVIT) in 2004. We enjoy our retirement—traveling with the 5th-wheel, spending time with family (10 grandchildren, 3 great-grands), bowling, reading, knitting, cooking and scrap-booking.

I've written a "neighborhood" column for the Mesa Tribune, (I had illusions of being another Erma Bombeck!) Various "Letters to the Editor"; poems published in "The MesaAgenda" for Mesa Public School employees and church newsletter; edited and published the EVITEA newsletter and wrote some PR articles for EVIT

FACEBOOK: Marchelle Perry

GOD, MY HONDA & MY SEAT BELT SAVED MY LIFE
A True Account
By Carol Farris

Just after 4:00 P.M. I dropped my friend, Sheila off after an afternoon of Bunco. Sitting at the red light a block from her house, I made a last minute decision to go straight through the intersection and go to the grocery store instead of turning left to go home.

The light turned green. Almost through the intersection, in my peripheral vision I saw a flash—a speeding car crashed into me sending my car airborne.

My car landed on its top facing the opposite direction. I hung there upside down, held securely by my seat belt.

I have to get out of here before the car starts on fire. I sniffed but didn't smell a fuel leak. The driver's door wouldn't open. I would drop on my head if the seat belt released me but my fear of fire was more powerful than common sense so—I kept trying but couldn't release my seat belt.

Terrified, alone, and unable to free myself, I began pleading out loud, "Dear Jesus, help me! Please Jesus, help me! Jesus, please help me!" Each petition was more desperate and more intense. *Is He there? Is He hearing me?*

In the next second I heard a voice ask, "Are you okay Ma'am?" A man sounded like he was inside my car.

Jesus did send help. Thank you Jesus!

"Yes, I'm okay," I answered.

"Don't worry, ma'am we'll get you out of here. We've already called 911," the voice of an angel responded. He kept talking to me and reassuring me. *He doesn't sound worried. I guess I won't worry either.* He had seen my car from the outside and would know if there was any smoke. My gas tank was nearly full.

This angel, who must have been sent from God, made his way to me so I could finally connect a face with his voice. Such a kind face! His slender stature enabled him to fit between the upside down headrests to reach me.

Another man, who I never did see, communicated with my angel from outside the car. They both agreed my seatbelt would have to be cut. A resident went into his house for a pair of super-duty scissors to cut me loose.

My angel, lying now on the ceiling of my inverted car, placed his arm and his shoulder under me so that when I fell, I would gently roll onto him and not be injured when they cut the seatbelt.

Finally, almost free, the man outside started pulling me slowly out the passenger door. Oops, wait! My foot was stuck. It was tangled in the steering wheel, which seemed to be in the back seat, but upside down, everything seemed confusing.

My angel told me later he expected my foot to be broken because of how it was entwined in the steering wheel. It wasn't.

A little more pulling got me out of the car. Someone brought a folded blanket so I didn't have to sit directly on the street. The sirens sounded closer now. A kind woman, a nurse, asked if I could move my neck. I could.

The firemen and first responders tended to me. Blood oozed from my wrist because of a cut from my watch. Somehow, while my hand was bent backward, it pressed into my arm until it drew blood. My hair had blood in it but it must have come from my wrist. There were no other cuts.

Two handsome firemen helped me stand but held onto me. One asked, "Do you think you can stand on your own?" Internally an earthquake was going on in my body. I didn't want them to let go. Would I fall? Maybe.

They checked me over and after a couple of hours, determined I could be released. As we walked out of ER my nurse said, "Heaven's angels were with you this afternoon."

Days later, I talked to my very own personal angel, Ronald, who along with his sister, Marsha, had been waiting at that light, intending to turn left after I navigated through the intersection. Unlike most drivers, they didn't venture into the intersection. They saw the car speeding toward me and watched in horror as the impact sent my car into the air. According to Marsha, they sat spellbound as my car flipped twice and then twisted, coming to rest on its top. Convinced that my car would land on their car, killing them, they were saying their good-byes. Marsha said, "I thought this would be the day I join my husband in heaven, He's been dead for twelve years."

My car didn't touch theirs. They were safe. Ronald, a retired EMT jumped into action. Bounding out of their car he yelled to the man in the car behind him, "Call 911." He rushed to my driver's side door. It was jammed. The back seat window was shattered. He pushed it in, opened the side door and crawled into the car. His was the voice I came to know as my angel.

A slightly built, retired, EMT, whose sister said they don't normally travel on that road, was right there when I needed him. A coincidence? I don't believe in coincidences.

As I sat on the road, the officers asked if there was anyone I wanted to call. I wished I could call my dog, Maggie, and say, "Don't worry baby. I'm going to be a little late getting home."

I called Sheila, who I had just dropped off. She and her husband, Art walked down to the corner. Sheila saw the car before she saw me. "I expected to see a lot of blood," she said. Once she and Art knew I would be transported by ambulance, they took my garage door opener to go let Maggie out. They also called our minister to tell him of my accident. The three of them, Dr. Steve, Art and Sheila, came to the ER and stayed with me while I got checked over. Once released, Art and Sheila took me home and helped me call my insurance company. I would need a rental car right away.

My car was totaled. Enterprise didn't have a Honda CRV and I wouldn't drive any of the little cracker boxes on their line. So they showed me a brand new Chrysler 300. It resembled a tank. "I'll take that one."

My insurance agent instructed me to get the license plate from my car. How would seeing my car affect me? Except for the smashed doors and shattered windshield and windows, the car stood tall. Shivers turned to goose bumps.

Only the passenger door would open. I reached in to get my house key off my key ring. The shoes I intended to donate were scattered about the car and the Chico's shopping bag they were in was badly torn. Unable and unwilling to crawl inside the car, I sadly left the shoes to be crushed with the car.

The day after the accident, Sheila told me she had the phone number for Ronald's sister. I could call them and get the answers to my many questions. "Yes, I want to call them." But, as I reached for the phone and thought about talking to him, I cried. Every time I pictured having a conversation with my angel, tears flowed and I wept uncontrollably. *I'll wait another day to call him and hopefully get some control of my emotions.*

A week later we finally met, I learned that Ronald was more than a little worried about the car starting on fire. It must have been his EMT training that helped him sound comforting and reassuring. How brave of him to be in the car with me, not sure if it would suddenly burst into flames. I got through our lunch meeting with just a couple of instances of a cracked voice. Emotional healing had begun.

Driving after the accident became torturous. Yet, I knew I must drive. My shoulders tightened at every intersection as if bracing for what may be coming. If any car moved unexpectedly, I cringed. It didn't matter if I was driving or a passenger. My hearing was severely affected in the accident. Chiropractic appointments fixed some whiplash, my sore back, knee and foot in due time.

Professionals agreed an accident like mine would have killed most drivers or at least resulted in a broken neck or back. My unbroken body is a miracle. I am a miracle.

The sturdiness of my Honda with its plethora of airbags, the fortitude of my seat belt, which forcefully protected me until help arrived, aided in my survival. They were part of my miracle.

But, I realize being in a car that soared through the air, flipped, and then flipped again, twisting and finally landing on its roof, meant that angels, several of them were surrounding me, were cushioning me, and were protecting me. Not only did the angels protect me that day, they protected Ronald and Marsha.

Why did God let the accident happen at all? I don't know. Perhaps if the speeder, who claimed the sun blinded him, hadn't hit me, he might have done more damage to someone not in the company of angels.

At the very least I will tell the story of God's miraculous works to everyone who will read this story. Maybe that's what He has planned for me.

More About Carol—

Most of Carol's working career was in retail sales. With an A.A. Degree in Supervisory Management earned later in life, several rewarding management jobs followed.

Being single for thirty years between marriages, with God's help, Carol raised her children by herself. Other life experiences such as breast cancer, the sudden death of her husband, and a terrible car accident, have all impacted her life. All have contributed to a never ending supply of stories of survival and inspiration. Today both children are successful adults, wonderful parents in great marriages. Now retired, Carol has recently moved to be closer to their families, and all six grandchildren. She will now have plenty of time and material to write more memoirs.

Facebook - www.facebook.com/carolfarris2.

Other publications include Christmas at Grandma's published by Little Cab Press and a tri-fold brochure, "If your spouse dies suddenly at home...What no one else will tell you." The local first responders include a copy in all of their code folders.

MAYA AND THE MESSIAH
By A.P. Maddox

John 10:16
And other sheep I have, which are not of this fold:
them also I must bring,
and they shall hear my voice;
and there shall be one fold, and one shepherd.

It was a bright, sunny morning as seven-year old Maya hobbled out of the hut with her walking stick to greet the day. Maya had been born with a twisted leg and could only walk with the help of her stick. She closed her eyes and stretched her neck out toward the sun, letting her smiling face soak up the rays.

Her mother emerged from the hut with Maya's two younger brothers in tow and her baby sister on her back—the boys each carrying large, empty pots for water. They made their way down to the river, the boys hefting the pots and Maya trailing her mother, making funny faces at her sister to make her laugh.

They got to the river and met up with Maya's father, who was fishing for the food they, and other villagers, would eat for the next few days. Other fathers worked the fields bringing in the crops while still others tended flocks of sheep and goats. Everyone had a job in Maya's village. Maya's job was to help tend her brothers and baby sister and help her mother around the hut with the cooking and the cleaning.

Maya loved her family and her life but every once in a while she wondered how much more she could do if her leg was more like other children's legs.

After filling the pots with the water their family would need for a couple of days and helping their father fill their large baskets with fish, they carried them back to the village. Maya and her five-year old brother tagged along with their father as he went to trade their excess fish for crops and other goods their family would need.

Soon her brother saw some neighbor friends and ran off to play with them. She followed after, but much slower. She sat on a rock and giggled as she watched them race each other, play tag and play with sticks and rocks. One friend would toss a rock to the other and the other would hit it with a stick. They all took turns and measured how far each of the rocks had gone, the one who hit the rock the farthest was the victor. Everyone cheered for the victor!

They ran off to play another game in another part of the village but Maya stayed on her rock. She used the tip of her walking stick to draw in the dirt. Maya drew in the dirt often to pass the time and had become quite good at it. She drew a jaguar—though she had only ever seen one once in her life—when it had stalked into the village. It gave the mothers a fright as they gathered their children into their huts. The fathers took up their bows, arrows and spears and killed the intruder—knowing if they let it go, it may return.

"What are you doing?" asked a twelve-year old neighbor boy named Emron, coming to sit next to her.

"I'm making a picture of a jaguar," she replied looking up to greet him with a smile.

"It's very good," he told her. "I've seen a few in the distance when I've been out working the fields. I always pray they won't come too near the village."

Maya nodded in agreement. "I like to make pictures with my stick," she added. "It keeps my mind of off..." Her voice trailed off.

"Off of your leg?" he asked slowly.

Maya nodded again. "I can't run and play games with the others," she said with a shrug.

Emron nodded his understanding and put his hand on her shoulder to comfort her.

"Still," she said perking up, "I have lots of things to make me happy. I love my family and they love me and God gave us this beautiful place to live in and the people of our village have always been kind to me!"

Emron quickly agreed. "Yes, they've always been kind to my family too, especially after my mother lost her sight and my father died in the war. Our neighbors have always made sure we have food and all the things we need. Your father is especially helpful. My brother has now taken a wife of his own and moved out of our hut, so it falls on me to take care of my mother. Without your father's help it would be much harder. I am very grateful to him."

Emron's father had recently gone to war with many of the other men of the village when a neighboring village tried to enslave theirs. Not too many of their men had been lost, for they had been victorious against their neighbor, but Emron's father was one of the few.

Maya beamed a smile, she knew her father had been very helpful to their neighbors and friends in need and she was very proud of him.

"Maya," her mother's voice called. "It is time to pick the herbs."

Maya jumped up, placing her stick securely under her arm. "Coming," she called back joyfully. "I'll see you later at the gathering," she told Emron, waving her good-byes.

Gathering herbs was something Maya could do very easily, for she could sit to do it. She went with her mother and the other village mothers and daughters to the large herb garden they had all planted months earlier, to gather up the herbs and dry them for storage for the upcoming season.

Later that afternoon many of the village families gathered in the village center—a large outdoor amphitheater where they could sit and face the elders as they spoke. One of the elders stood and came to the middle to address those in attendance.

"We are grateful to our God for our bounteous harvest," he began. It was the time of year when the crops were ripe in the field and being gathered, fruits of the forest were being collected and fish and meat were plentiful. They had come to the gathering to give thanks to the creator of all things.

The elder continued. "Our fathers came to this land many hundreds of years ago. They were called out of the land of their inheritance by the voice of God before that time when their great city was to be destroyed. They were preserved from destruction by the hand of God to preserve among them the word of God. They were led to this new and promised land. They preached of the coming of a Messiah— one who would redeem all mankind from sin. When I was a younger man and had just started a family of my own I witnessed the sign of this Messiah's birth. I saw the night with no darkness. The sun went down but it did not get dark and the next morning we knew that on that day, the Messiah, the Christ child would be born in the land our fathers had left. I also saw the new star appear in the sky—just as our fathers had prophesied it would."

Many of the elder grandfathers and grandmothers nodded their heads and voiced their testimonies of seeing the signs of the Messiah's birth.

"Now," he went on, "We watch for the signs of his death and resurrection from death."

At that moment, a younger man jumped up from the crowd and went toward the center to interrupt the elder. "How long are we going to continue hearing these stories?" he asked, swinging his arms wide as if inviting all to listen to him instead of the elder. "I wasn't there, I did not see the sign, nor did most of the people in this gathering. How do we know the elders aren't making these stories up to keep us under their thumbs?"

Many of the younger men and women applauded the man and shouted their dissentions to the elder's stories.

Maya gasped and brought her hand to her mouth. "Isn't that your brother?" She whispered to Emron, seated next to her.

With a look which encompassed shock, despondency and embarrassment, Emron slowly nodded that it was. "I'm sorry," he said quietly. "His opinion is not that of my mother's or my own—we believe!"

Emron's mother, seated on the other side of him, reached out her hand looking for his. He clasped it and held it tightly.

"Though my eyes cannot see," Emron's mother said, "my ears can hear the voice of my eldest son and my heart is filled with sorrow for his soul."

Emron leaned over and kissed her cheek. "It is okay mother," he said. "The sacrifice of the Messiah will redeem even the non-believers, though their reward in heaven will not be as great as the believers."

"Bless you my son," she replied, as a tear escaped down her cheek.

The elder spoke up again in a louder voice. "The time draws near; we will very soon see the sign of the Messiah's death—three days of darkness!"

"Won't happen!" The younger man mocked, drawing laughs from the non-believers.

"Repent and believe." The elder warned.

"My father died to preserve our freedom and I choose to use my freedom to not believe," the younger man stated firmly. He motioned for the other non-believers to follow him and they left the village center.

The elder sighed and sadly shook his head. He then drew forth a record and opened it and began reading the ancient prophesies about the Messiah to those who remained.

Maya's father was a believer and had taught his family to believe, and in that moment, she was thankful.

When they returned home for their evening meal, Maya thought aloud while setting dishes out. "Do you think if the Messiah were here, instead of in a land far away, do you think he could straighten my leg, so I could run and play, like the other children?"

Maya's parents stopped what they were doing, looked at each other and then looked at Maya with warm smiles. "Yes," Maya's father answered, coming close to kiss the top of her head, "I do think he would."

Maya continued placing dishes around the table, her walking stick carving a dotted circle in the dirt floor around the table. "Do you think he'd give Emron's mother her sight back?" she asked.

"Yes my darling child," Maya's father added, "I think he'd do that too."

Maya grinned, just the thought of such miracles made her smile.

The next morning was much the same in the village, everyone worked to bring in and preserve the food all would need for the coming season. The non-believers however, had decided to go around the village preaching that the elders had fooled everyone, that there was no Messiah and it was foolish to continue looking for signs and believing in old wives' tales.

The elder, who had spoken the previous evening, followed them, telling the people not to listen, but to have faith and believe. He testified again he had seen the signs of the Messiah's birth and he knew he had been born and that he lived.

This made the non-believers angry and soon they began to pick up stones and started throwing them at the elder. Emron ran to his brother and grabbed his arm, trying to make him stop. And though Emron was strong for a twelve-year old, his brother hit him with his other hand, knocking him to the ground. Many of the stones hit the elder and one even hit him in the head before the other villagers were able to stop them and chase them out of the village—warning them not to come back.

Emron was helped up and, showing no signs of serious injury, he returned to his mother.

The elder was taken to his hut and cared for but it wasn't certain he'd survive.

Later in the day a large storm began. It thundered and lightning struck, then it thundered some more and the lightening got worse and then whirlwinds came and the earth started to tremble.

Maya's dad stood at the door, looking out. "I've never seen a storm like this before. The lightening is striking everywhere, all at once and the thunder is so loud and constant we can hardly hear each other," he said.

Maya's mother had a worried look on her face. "Should we head for the caves?" she asked.

Her father nodded. "Yes I believe we should," he answered.

They quickly gathered up some emergency supplies and stepped out into the storm to head for the safety of the caves. They were not alone in in this decision for most of the village was also headed to the caves. The wind was so strong they had to hold onto each other tight. Emron and his mother had come out of their hut at about the same time. The two families held onto and helped each other along. Maya could see the injured elder being carried and she hoped he would be alright.

Off in the distance they could see entire neighboring villages consumed in flames—they had been struck by the continuous lightening. As they got to the safety of the caves, which were elevated higher than their village, they looked out over the landscape. There were holes in the earth where there used to be mountains, there were mountains where there used to be flat ground and there was smoke everywhere from the fires that were burning the villages—and still the storm raged on. They looked back down on their own village, most of the huts had been torn apart by the wind and some of their friends and neighbors hadn't made it to the caves alive.

The villagers were scared, there was chatter throughout the caves that even the elders had never seen such a vicious storm. It began to get dark and many of the fathers tried to start fires for their families but their efforts were fruitless, fires would not start, torches would not stay lit, not one flame persisted.

Maya's and Emron's families huddled close to each other. The darkness got darker—unlike a moonless night—the darkness was thick and heavy. They could not see the moon or the stars or even their hands in front of their faces.

"Everything will be fine in the morning," Maya's dad whispered, holding his family close.

But long hours passed and when it seemed the morning should be approaching and the sun should be rising, the darkness persisted. Again, some tried to start fires, to no avail.

"What is happening father?" Maya asked.

"I'm not sure," he replied.

Then came an elderly voice from the back of the cave. "Three days of darkness...three days of darkness."

Whisperings erupted throughout the cave. "It's just as the elders said, three days of darkness."

"Is that what it is father?" Maya asked.

"It's possible," he replied.

"Will we be okay?" she asked.

"Of course we will," he reassured her.

She felt his hand stroke her hair to comfort her. Her baby sister cried in the darkness but her mother quickly comforted and quieted her. Maya and her brothers sat between their mother and father, everyone huddled very close.

As people began to realize what might be happening—that this could be the sign of the Messiah's death—they began to cry for those who had perished in the storm. Some had family members and neighbors who had perished. They had witnessed whole villages burning.

"If only they had repented and believed," they wailed.

Maya's and Emron's families sat so close in a semi-circle, Maya could feel Emron's feet near hers. His mother cried with a soft voice, "I just know my son is no more!"

Maya could hear Emron trying to comfort her. "It's alright mother, everything will be alright."

People cried and wailed as the darkness persisted. Long hours passed and seemed to run together. Maya started to wonder if the darkness would ever end. It felt as though it was lasting much longer than three days.

"Hasn't it been three days yet father?" she asked.

"I don't think so, but it's hard to tell when we have no way to keep track of the time in this thick darkness," he said.

Everyone felt the time drag on—it seemed never ending. The wailing and crying grew louder. They cried in sorrow for their own sins, in grief for the wickedness of lost loved ones and for their present condition. Great became their cries of anguish.

They heard crying in the distance as well, survivors from other villages, languishing also. So loud were there cries together, that Maya thought, surely they must all be heard all the way up to the heavens, by God himself. She covered her ears, trying to drown out the sound.

Then as if her mind was being read, a calm, yet authoritative voice coming from the heavens spoke. It cried unto the people that they must repent! It told them that most of the villages throughout all the face of the land had been destroyed and most of the inhabitants destroyed also because of their disbelief and wickedness. The voice declared that those who were spared had been more faithful than those who had been destroyed.

Then the voice declared unto them that he was the Messiah—the Savior and Redeemer—the Son of God—Jesus Christ the Lord! He told them that by him all things were created. He declared he had come into the world to bring redemption to all the world and to save the world from sin— and for this purpose he had laid down his life and had taken it up again. Then he told them to repent and come unto him and be saved.

After the voice had spoken there was silence— no more crying, no more wailing—but silence! For when the people heard these words—they were so astonished, they ceased their crying and wailings and they sat in silence for many hours.

After a time, the voice of the Lord came to them again, telling them he had come to gather them as a hen gathers her chicks and then suddenly the darkness began to disperse and the light of the morning shone through and the people rejoiced and praised their Lord and Redeemer, Jesus Christ.

They emerged from their caves and went in search of the other survivors, for they had heard their lamenting cries in the darkness. The elder, who had been stoned, had survived the days of darkness and was carried among them also.

"Father, our hut is gone," Maya said as they walked through the remains of their village.

Maya's father clutched her hand with one hand and held her frightened three-year old brother in his other arm. Her mother carried her baby sister on her back and held tightly to her oldest son's hand. Emron had his mother's arm looped through his as he guided her along.

"Yes, Maya, most of our village has been destroyed," Maya's father replied.

"What will we do now?" she asked.

"We must find others," he said. "We must all band together now, for survival." They trudged forward with the others of their village and he added, "And we must heed the voice of the Lord and repent and come unto him."

"How do we do that Father?" she asked.

"Through prayer, Maya, we must pray like we've never prayed before. And obey, we must obey and have faith," he said.

They continued on and soon passed a large boulder; under it, the corner of a cloak was sticking out. Emron recognized the cloak as his brother's and realized his brother was under the boulder too, smashed, along with the cloak. His heart felt a deep sorrow for his brother but he said nothing to his mother, not wanting to add to her grief.

People from other villages throughout the land had also gone in search of survivors and soon they all found each other and gathered themselves together in a great multitude—regardless of their tribe—they gathered together. They looked over the destruction that lay all throughout the land and marveled at their survival.

They began to relate to each other the voice they had heard from the heavens—the voice of their Lord and Redeemer Jesus Christ—and soon realized they had all heard the same voice speak the same words.

While telling each other these things, they heard again another voice coming from the heavens saying, "Behold my Beloved Son, in whom I am well pleased, in whom I have glorified my name—hear ye him!"

They looked up—heavenward to the direction from whence the voice came and they saw a man descending out of the heavens, dressed in glorious white robes, whiter than any whiteness they had ever before beheld. He descended slowly until finally he came to stand among them.

They looked upon him and there was silence again, none spoke, not even to each other. Finally he spoke to them and stretched forth his hands toward them and told them again that he was Jesus Christ, the Messiah whom the prophets had testified would come and after he said this, they fell down, all of them, upon the ground.

He told them to arise and come forth unto him and feel the nail prints in his hands and feet and to feel the spear wound in his side—so they would know he was the God of Israel, the God of the whole earth, who had been slain for the sins of the world.

They arose and did go forth, each one, until one by one—each father, mother, elder and child had felt and saw and witnessed that it was he whom the prophets had said would come. When they had finished they all cried with one voice, "Hosanna! Blessed be the name of the Most High God!" And they knelt at his feet and worshipped him.

When they arose again he taught them his gospel and gave them commandments and told them to keep his commandments continually and to serve the Lord and to love one another. He taught them to pray and commanded them to fast.

After he taught them many great things, he called for the sick and the lame, the deaf and the blind and all who were infirmed to be brought forward unto him so that he could bless and heal them.

The elder was brought first. His breath was slow and his eyes were closed and he was near to death. The Lord placed his hands on his head and commanded him to be healed and in that moment the elder opened his eyes, drew a strong breath and came to his feet before his Lord. He cried, and thanked the Lord and worshipped at his feet. Then others were brought and each were healed.

Maya's turn soon came and she asked her father to pick her up in his arms and to carry her. She gave her mother her walking stick and told her, "I won't need this anymore."

Her father carried her to the Lord and as he held her there the Lord placed his hands on her head and commanded Maya to be healed. When he had spoken these words, her dad put her down on her own feet and she looked at her legs, both were straight and whole! She ran to her mother and hugged her, then ran back to her father and hugged him and then she knelt down before the Lord and thanked him with all her love. She looked up, into his face, and saw him looking back at her with all the love and tenderness of a gentle parent. Tears of gratitude fell from her eyes.

Next it was Emron's mother's turn. Emron guided her to the Lord. As she stood before him her frame shook with anticipation. It had been eight long years since her eyes beheld her family and the world around her. She had not been able to look upon her husband's face before he went off to the battle which took his life. She had felt his tender hug and his last kiss on her soft cheek but had not had the privilege of looking upon his face one last time. The last time she had seen Emron's face, he was a small child with the face of a babe. She had not beheld his face as he had grown into a young man.

The Lord placed his hands on her head and her shaking ceased and she was filled with faith. When he commanded her to be whole, she blinked several times, adjusting to the light then looked to her son who was still holding tightly to her arm.

"Emron!" she cried, placing her hands on his cheeks and looking over every detail of his face. "My beautiful son, I thought I'd never look upon your face again," she said, taking him in her arms and holding him tight as tears streamed down her face. They held each other, crying tears of joy.

Once all who had been afflicted had been healed, the multitude again worshipped the Lord, bathing his feet with their tears of gratitude.

He then called for the children to be brought to him—each child, every one—and one by one he laid his hands upon their heads and blessed each one.

Soon after the time came for him to go and the people were sad to see him leave and wished he could stay but he had taught and blessed them and they were prepared to go forward in faith, keeping the commandments and continually worshipping and obeying the Lord.

He slowly ascended to the heavens, glorious white light beaming all around him. They watched until they could see him no longer, then went about marveling about the glorious things they had seen and heard.

They helped each other rebuild, as one tribe and as one people and Maya's people lived in peace with no wars, battles, contentions or disputations among them for many, many generations.

Trust
By Carrington Bonner

This dark world we are living in
Don't let it hurt the person within
You hide it well, all the glory beneath,
This heavy rain will never you breach!

This clumsy life you pretend to lead
I know I am the one you need
Don't hold back this moment is ours
But take your time; we'll live in the stars!

You are strong, yes you are strong!

This rain coming down,
it may touch the ground,
But it won't touch me
If I plant my feet in you!
And I know who you are
You are the truth; I'll put my trust in you!

I know I have so much to live for
When I hear you knock at my door
I'll let you in, please hold me tight
When you're here I lose all my fright!

I'll be strong, you make me strong!

Where I was blind once, now I can see
I am only whole when you're here with me
I see a light taking over the darkness
It is white where once was all anguish!

You are bright, you are the light!

If I fall, stand me tall!
If I cry, teach me to fly!

We can fly! We can stand tall!

This rain coming down, it'll touch the ground,
But it can't touch me
When I plant my feet in you!
I know who you are
You are the truth; I put my trust in you!

Story Credits

WORTH OF A SOUL By A.P. Maddox copyright © 2016 by A.P. Maddox

BE STILL AND KNOW THAT I AM GOD By Bonnie Johnson copyright © 2016 by Bonnie Johnson

LOOSE THREADS By Kaine Thompson copyright © 2016 by Kaine Thompson

GET VERY FAR AWAY By Anne Marie Kensington copyright © 2016 Anne Marie Kensington

THE TINIEST TEACHER By Alice Klies copyright © 2016 by Alice Klies

KISSED BY KAYA By Liz Hufford copyright © 2016 by Liz Hufford

THE HUNT By Dianna Beamis Good copyright © 2016 Dianna Beamis Good

THE GOAT By Joshua Good copyright © 2016 by Joshua Good

THE TRIKE RIDE By Burton Voss copyright © 2016 by Burton Voss

THE HUALPAI By Roy Voss copyright © 2016 by Roy Voss

THE OBIT By Roy Voss copyright © 2016 by Roy Voss

THE UNEXPECTED By Mark Enlow copyright © 2016 by Mark Enlow

A LESSON IN TIME By Anne Marie Kensington copyright © 2016 by Anne Marie Kensington

GOOD WITCH VS BAD WITCH By Alice Klies copyright © 2016 by Alice Klies

KEEP ON KEEPING ON! By Marchelle Perry copyright © 2016 by Marchelle Perry

GOD, MY HONDA & MY SEAT BELT SAVED MY LIFE By Carol Farris copyright © 2016 by Carol Farris

MAYA AND THE MESSIAH By A.P. Maddox copyright © 2016 by A.P. Maddox

TRUST By Carrington Bonner copyright © 2016 by Carrington Bonner

Thank you for reading Little CAB Press's
2016 Spring Anthology

Please follow Little CAB Press at www.littlecabpress.com &
Like https://www.facebook.com/LittleCABpress

If you are a writer, please join us by submitting a story to one of our
upcoming anthologies-

Summer 2016 Anthology: Summer Fun Fiction; stories due June 30, 2016. For our summer anthology anything goes! All fiction welcome: Adventure, Contemporary, Fantasy (including folklore, fairy tale, myths, dragons etc), Historical (including Western, Regency, etc), Mystery (including whodunits, detective, thrillers, etc), Science Fiction (including space, aliens, superhero, etc). "Adult-only" content not accepted. Fiction should be at least 2,500 words but no more than 6,000; first chapters of novels, may be accepted.

2016 Christmas Anthology: Stories due September 1, 2016. We are looking for Christmas, Hanukkah, New Year's and Valentine's stories to inspire and entertain during the holiday season. These stories can be true accounts of wondrous, miraculous or even just comical holiday experiences or they can be fictional stories. Fiction should be at least 2,500 words but no more than 6,000, non-fiction should be at least 750 words but no more than 2,500.

Children's Holiday Book Project 2016: Stories due September 1, 2016. We are looking for Thanksgiving, Christmas, New Year's and Valentine's stories to inspire and entertain CHILDREN during the holiday season. These stories can be true accounts of wondrous, miraculous or even just comical holiday experiences or they can be fictional stories. True accounts must be written fictionalized. Stories may be as little as 100 words or up to 500 words and written for children ages 3-8. These stories will mostly be read by adults to children, so don't worry about using easy to read words for beginning readers. Characters can be animal or human but main characters should be young, let any adults in the story be supporting rather than main characters. The young characters should be driving the action in the story.
Art work: Upon acceptance authors must submit three pieces of art work (at their own expense) to go with their stories, the first to show the beginning action of the story, the second to show the middle action and the third to show the resolution action of the story. To the best of our ability we will place art work on the left page with text on the right page.

Visit www.littlecabpress.com for more info